THE UNSETTLED

THE UNSETTLED

I hope you enjoy a little glimpse into the past, xoxo with a splash of adventure.

'15

CHRISTINE ALLEY-GARCIA

AuthorHouse™
1663 Liberty Drive
Bloomington, IN 47403
www.authorhouse.com
Phone: 1-800-839-8640

© 2013 by Christine Alley-Garcia. All rights reserved.

No part of this book may be reproduced, stored in a retrieval system, or transmitted by any means without the written permission of the author.

Published by AuthorHouse 06/10/2013

ISBN: 978-1-4817-5055-4 (sc)
ISBN: 978-1-4817-5054-7 (hc)
ISBN: 978-1-4817-5053-0 (e)

Library of Congress Control Number: 2013908248

Any people depicted in stock imagery provided by Thinkstock are models, and such images are being used for illustrative purposes only.
Certain stock imagery © Thinkstock.

This book is printed on acid-free paper.

Because of the dynamic nature of the Internet, any web addresses or links contained in this book may have changed since publication and may no longer be valid. The views expressed in this work are solely those of the author and do not necessarily reflect the views of the publisher, and the publisher hereby disclaims any responsibility for them.

I dedicate this book to my beloved late grandparents, Evelyn and Baker, who will always be a part of my most fond childhood memories. And to my mother and father, Doris and Gene, who have always believed in me.

CONTENTS

Birthdays	1
The Funeral Home	7
The Secret	15
Ghost Stories	19
Grandmother's Wisdom	27
Investigating	32
Answers	37
Warning	43
The Aftermath	50
Saving Jane	55
A Forbidden Friend	65
Lost and Found	75
Goodbye for Now	85
Uninvited Guest	91
Forgotten	96
Going Home	102
The Other Jonathan	105
Searching the Heavens	111
Decoding the Message	124
Keeping the Secret	134
The Return Trip	141
Hiding Places	152
Decisions	158
Home	164
School	170

BIRTHDAYS

Ever since I can remember, I've been shipped off to live in Halls, Tennessee during my summer vacation. For two whole months, every summer, without fail, I was sent to "the farm" like an unwanted pet. At the time, I thought I was being tortured. I would tell my friends "good-bye" on the last day of school, with tear-stricken eyes, as if I was being sent to prison to serve a recurring two-month sentence.

Being forced to spend every summer in a town where people grew their own food, made a pie for every occasion, and pickled their own . . . everything, is barely tolerable when you're used to living in a big city like Scottsdale. I think my parents were hoping that by shipping me to the farm I would gain an appreciation for what it was like when they were growing up. Don't get me wrong, I do enjoy the stories about my great-grandmother's refusal to stop using the outhouse when indoor plumbing was invented. I even appreciate hearing about the time my father built a motorbike out of spare parts he salvaged while exploring abandoned farmhouses and junk heaps. However, I don't know how these events relate to my life or what they were supposed to 'teach' me. Maybe they were hoping I would understand the virtues of growing up without the modern conveniences that we take for granted today. All I knew for sure was that when all the kids at school were looking forward to their summer vacations, I was imaging how many bug bites I would have to smother with Calamine lotion.

My daily events quickly changed from hanging out at the mall with my best friend, searching for my next "true-love"; to cracking green beans on the back porch with a cousin whose idea of the "best birthday present ever" was a brown umbrella with scalloped edges suitable for a woman in her 80's.

Though it was always met with some resistance, the trips to Halls became part of my ordinary, mundane life. Nothing exciting ever happened to me anyway. This was at least a change of scenery. Since I wasn't the type of kid to sit and mope with despair about spending my summers abroad, I tried to make the best of my prison sentence by using my imagination to get me through the long humid days. Of course, there were only so many pennies you could flatten on the train tracks, and stray dogs you could rescue. A lot of my time was spent roaming the streets of Downtown Halls. There was no lack of people and places to feed my curiosities. Watching the old men playing checkers in front of Arnold's Drug Store, shooing away the kids that were trading comic books, was always a fun way to pass the time. I would often walk around and admire the old cars that cruised around the Town Square showing off a new paint job or hood ornament.

However, my favorite pastime, and what I looked forward to more than anything, was sifting through my grandparents' attic. They had boxes and boxes of antiquities that sparked my curiosity. It always felt like I was looking through forbidden treasure when I went up there. My heart would race a little bit whenever I climbed the stairs to the attic. The musty smell and dust particles in the air drew me in like a magnet. It was spooky and creepy and gave me goose bumps. Every time I pulled down the rickety staircase and began my ascent, the hairs on my neck would stand straight up. I'm not sure why I loved the thrill of the unknown dark secrets of the past so much, I guess they just made my trips more exciting.

My grandparents were well aware of my apprehension, especially since my birthday happened to be smack in the middle of summer. This meant that every birthday I ever had, since about the age of 7, I had the pleasure of spending my special day with my aged grandparents. I quickly realized that I had to come up with some ways to celebrate, other than with a special treat of peanut butter and banana sandwiches and a trip to the penny candy store. They were always happy to help me come up with some mini-adventures or at least attempt to throw me a party.

The first birthday I ever spent there was when I turned 9 years old. This was the year that we drove for an hour "into town" to find a store where my dowdy grandmother fought through crowds to procure the sacred Cabbage Patch Kid doll I wanted for my birthday present. I watched with amusement as my grandmother shuffled around and wrestled this big box away from another crazed woman. She maneuvered her way through the crowd to the store window and held up a doll just like the one I described to her and yelled to me, "Samantha, is this here the one ya want?"

My grandmother was a genuine southern woman. Her arms were the size of ham hocks, her dresses were homemade, and her heart was as big as the moon. She had no idea what this odd looking doll was, or why we had to get to the store before it opened to get one, but she did it, probably hoping it would keep me happy and out of trouble. She treated a trip into town like a Sunday dinner invitation. She would dress in her nicest outfit and wear her high-heels and lipstick. She always said, "Ya never go into town without some color on your lips." My grandfather liked to wash and wax his car before we went into town. As for myself, well, I just wore clothes that weren't cutoff jeans and shoes that had no holes. I felt like if I didn't dress up I would look like a farmhand that they picked up off the street on their way into town.

The next birthday my grandfather tried to make me a "slip-n-slide" out of his old tractor tarp, and invited all three of the neighbor kids over, none of which owned a bathing suit. He was very excited about his rendition of the slide and smiled with delight as we all tried to slip around on this thing. He realized the kids were having some trouble slipping around in their cut-off jeans and said, "why don't I fetch you some of grandmother's lard to grease it up a bit. That would make ya'll slip and slide straight into the train tracks!" We kindly declined his offer and made do with some dish soap lubricant.

My grandfather, whom all of my cousins and I lovingly called 'Granddaddy', was always messing around. My favorite thing about him was the noises he would make at the dinner table. He would quack like a duck with the corner of his mouth and then look around like, "Who did that?" He was pretty fun, for a Granddaddy. He smelled like an old cigar and always had one in his front pocket. He would chew on it, unlit, in the house all day. Then the minute he went outside, he lit up his cigar and smiled as he yanked on his suspenders. He always saved the cigar boxes for me. Every summer I would get to pick one out and use it for knick-knacks. I would put all of my drug store treasures in it, along with some squished pennies and anything I found that looked interesting. One year I found a bullet casing while digging up some potatoes from the garden, which Granddaddy said was likely from the Civil War.

My favorite treasure that was kept in my cigar box was an old photo of a grandfather clock with a ghostly face in it; I found it in their attic. When I asked what they thought it could be, their answers were vague. I must have showed that picture to anyone who would look at it. I was determined to have someone tell me it was a ghost. The face was distorted like when you look in a mirror at a funhouse; it was gray and almost transparent. The mouth was wide open, as if it was screaming. It was the spookiest thing I had ever seen, and it was my first piece of solid proof that ghosts must exist.

By the time my next summer trip rolled around, I discovered that my cousin Gabe, the one with the umbrella, lived on the rich side of town in a gorgeous, old fashioned, plantation-style house with an above ground pool. How it took me so long to find out this little gem is beyond me. Nevertheless, that big creepy, exciting house became the site of the last birthday party I ever celebrated in Tennessee, my 14th, and the mysterious subject of my overactive imagination.

THE FUNERAL HOME

Gabe's house was big and white and screamed for attention. It was at the end of a long driveway and had a grand entrance. The windows were adorned with brown shutters and the door was a huge, wood-carved masterpiece. It sat on a large piece of land that had thick trees in the back and several barns or garages spread about. It fit my Uncle Lee, who fancied himself as the unofficial Town Mayor, perfectly.

Gabe's family was very likeable, almost cookie-cutter from the outside. His mom, my aunt, was tall and thin and always dressed up like she was about to go to lunch with someone important. That's why I could never understand why people seemed to whisper and change their expressions when they turned their backs. That is, until I found out that Gabe's beautiful white house, with mahogany banisters, three stories, and multiple rooms was actually a converted funeral home. This was apparently the big secret that everyone whispered about. I started to look at the house very differently.

Once the secret was revealed, Gabe took no time filling me in on the former inter-workings of the home. One night when my grandparents and I went there for dinner, Gabe and I decided to go see the room where the bodies would be laid out and embalming occurred. It was deep within the basement, a place I never wanted to go. The farthest I had ever been was half way down the stairway. Gabe said he used to go down all the time when he was younger, but it had been years since he went in very far. This time we were both determined to go all the way in. As we started down the stairs, I held on to the back of Gabe's t-shirt with a tight grip. With every step we took, the creaking of the stairs became louder and louder, like they were fashioned to be an alarm system, alerting anything that needed to hide that intruders were on their way down. The light for the basement was at the end of the staircase and when Gabe went to flip the switch, a flash of light burst on and with a "pop", they turned out again, leaving nothing but a faint amber glow where a light should be.

"Oh great, the bulbs burnt out." Gabe whispered. "Should I go get my flashlight from my bedroom?"

"You're not leaving me here!" I said as I grasped his shirt tighter.

"There's another light switch at the other end of the basement. Should we make our way over there and try it?" Gabe said as he stood as frozen as I was.

We agreed and started shuffling over. The basement was huge and filled with large sheet covered masses. I had no idea what lie beneath the sheets, but my imagination was sure going on overdrive trying to figure it out. When we reached the other light switch, we had to move a large object out of the way to get to it. Thinking it would be heavy we prepared to use all of our might to push this contraption. As soon as Gabe gave it a shove, it started to roll. It looked like it was floating and again we were both frozen stiff watching where it was going. I must have been standing on the corner of the sheet that covered it because as it rolled the sheet stayed in place, slowly sliding off the object. It was darker in this part of the basement, but the object being revealed looked a lot like a casket. Gabe jerked quickly toward the light switch making me lose my grip on his shirt. I never took my eyes off of this rolling object.

Just as Gabe flipped the switch, the casket, which was fully uncovered now, slammed into something propped against the wall and the lid popped open. We both screamed and started running. I tripped over something and fell face first, but got right back up and kept running. When we reached the top of the stairs Gabe slammed the door shut and we continued running until we were safe outside of the house. We were panting, our eyes were bulging, and we looked at each other and just started laughing like crazy. That was the scariest moment I had ever experienced, yet it was exhilarating at the same time.

After that day, we explored every inch of that house. It was somewhat surprising to me that he hadn't already explored some of the nooks and crannies that we would find together. As scared as I was, and as hard as my heart would pound whenever I would be in this creepy house of death, I somehow could push my thoughts away long enough to satisfy my curiosities.

Although we spent days upon days playing detectives in his house, he never let me in to the room that was always locked. The room that was just at the top of the long winding stairs. I used to think it was some enormous linen closet and was just too unimportant to bother with. Once the rest of the house became a little less of a mystery, I really began to get curious about that locked room. My imagination would run wild every time I went over there. The fact that it was the room right next to Gabe's and he seemed to almost purposefully walk as far away from the door as he could when he passed by made it even harder to resist. I began conjuring up possible scenarios for what could lie within that locked room. Was it a storage locker with frozen bodies hidden in the walls? Was it covered with pictures of the deceased that had graced the presence of this once fine funeral home?

I was definitely one of those kids that feared death in a way that was almost blasphemous. See, my parents were religious in the sense that we went to church and went to bible school, but we were only "church folks" for a few hours on Sunday mornings. We didn't read passages or try to convert our neighbors. We simply believed that good people follow the golden rules, and went to heaven when they were old and died.

Death was a subject that haunted me since I was five and I had a nightmare that I was being eaten by a giant ice cream cone. Even at such a young age, I winced at the thought of death. Almost every night I would have a nightmare in which I was at the brink of death. Then I would wake up scared and sweaty.

Questions like, "What happens when you die?" and, "What is eternity going to feel like?" were always rattling around in my mind. Death to me is unimaginable. Forever seemed too long. How do we know what comes next after death? Don't we study Greek mythology and laugh at their ideas of Gods and Goddesses? I am just so confused about death. I tried to explain my fear of death and confusion about what happens in the after-life to anyone who would listen, but often received the typical response from adults: "Death is a part of life, sweetie."

I guess that's why I always had an odd fixation with ghosts. I feared them like cats feared water, but I desperately wanted to know if they were real. I had absolutely no experience with death so I had to use my imagination. I would hear ghost stories and the hair on my neck would stand straight up, but I would keep listening. My curiosity was overwhelming when it came to the thought of entities running loose in people's houses. I would eavesdrop on my parents' friends as they spoke about the Native American spirits that haunted their house. Could all of this be true? And if this were true, then, how would you know if you were going to be allowed to stay back and pull people's pictures off the wall, and make things shake and rattle when you died, or if you were going to go float on a cloud somewhere in a magical land? I really was hoping to find the answers to those questions at Gabe's house.

The mystery of that locked room at the top of the stairs was really consuming my thoughts. Sometimes my imagination would run wild as I walked the nearly two miles to Gabe's house. As I imagined what might be hiding behind the locked door, my heart would pound so hard in my chest with the thoughts of death and spirits filling my head that I would turn around and run back to my grandparents' house. There were even a couple of days where I would become paralyzed with the fear that the ghost of some previous client was wandering their hallways, and I would freeze at the top of the porch stairs with my eyes closed. My aunt thought I was very peculiar and wasn't sure I should be coming to the house so much.

I decided that I really needed to know everything Gabe knew, and believed, about death and ghosts. He must have some answers, seeing as he lives in a house of death. I needed to know if there were any ghosts in his house. If ghosts really did exist, then this would be the place to find them. Unfortunately, he was not at all interested in my curiosities. Especially when I relentlessly pleaded with him to show me what was behind the locked door. That was when he finally told me to leave. Once again, I was forced to leave my questions unanswered and let my imaginations go to work.

It wasn't until two weeks later, when a family celebration forced us to get together, that I was able to go back to Gabe's house. Great Aunt Winifred was turning 90 and Gabe's house was the only one suitable for a large gathering of large southerners. Aunt Winifred was a crazy old woman in my eyes. Every time I would pass by her house, she would suddenly appear out of nowhere and grab a hold of me. She would touch me and say, "You're the Alley girl ain't ya?" I always tried to avoid looking at her too closely. She only had about five teeth and she had a huge mole above her lip that had long whisker-like hair growing out of it. She was quite unfortunate looking.

On the way over to his house, we stopped by and picked up a family friend, Penny, who happened to be one of those women who had nothing better to do than gossip about the "goings-on" of Halls. She started in on my cousin's family and Grandmother shot her a look of disapproval, but not before she said, from the corner of her mouth, "people just can't understand how they could stay in that house after . . . . the accident."

Before I had a chance to ask the millions of questions that suddenly swelled inside my brain, my grandfather stopped the car in front of Gabe's big white intimidating house and everyone got out. Could there be more to the secret than I could have possibly imagined? Did the whispers surrounding this family have nothing to do with the fact that they lived in a funeral home? I had to find out what Penny was talking about.

THE SECRET

I decided to follow Penny, the town gossip, around the party and listen to her conversations. I was getting bored listening to her ramble on about some family nearby that apparently stopped going to the local church. She was asking everyone if they knew why they were no longer in attendance. Apparently, those folks were questioning their faith after some recent misfortune.

Then the conversation turned to the misfortunes of Gabe's family. My ears perked up and I began to really listen. I soon found out that the picture of the cute little boy that sat on the table in the hallway of the big, white, converted funeral home was of a cousin I had never had the chance to meet. This was Kenny, Gabe's older brother. I had always admired the picture, but assumed it was Gabe. They both had the same sandy blonde hair, ear-to-ear smile, and big blue eyes. The only difference was that Gabe wore glasses since he was about three and this boy seemed to be a bit older and did not have glasses on. She spoke about how young he was and what a tragedy it was, but I wasn't sure what had happened. Then I heard the words, "What a horrible way to die, and right here at home, such a shame." I couldn't believe my ears.

I always avoided anything that had to do with death, but I wondered how I didn't find out about this unknown cousin before today. My thoughts suddenly turned to poor Gabe. I began to look at my cousin sympathetically; he was the first person I had ever known that actually experienced a death in the family. I searched the house until I found Gabe sitting at the bottom of the stairs, trying to decide if he was still mad at me for being such a nuisance last time we hung out.

The picture sat near the stairway so I wandered over there and held it up, examining it so that he could see what I was doing. I had hoped he would start the conversation.

"Did your parents tell you how he died?" I asked, hoping not to make him upset, but desperately wanting to know the answer.

"Yes, but I don't really like to talk about it too much. I'm surprised you haven't found out after all these years, as curious as you are," Gabe said, avoiding my gaze. He told me he didn't really know his brother because Kenny died one month and one day before Gabe was born. He went on to explain that Kenny was almost five when he died and it happened one year after they moved into the big white house. To my surprise, Gabe continued divulging information without me even prompting him. I guess he kept this information bottled up inside of him for too long.

We decided to hide in his room to avoid the party downstairs. In his room there was a huge closet with a door that was hidden behind his clothes and an old train set. I noticed once when we played hide and seek but never dared to even touch the doorknob. He asked me to go inside and I did. The door led to a short staircase, which led into his attic, but it didn't look like the attics I had seen. There were no dusty old boxes or covered furniture. It was completely bare, with unpolished wooden floors and one small window at the end of the room. He led me to the window, which faced his backyard. We could see the partygoers, his pool, and the tops of the trees that were behind his yard.

There, Gabe explained to me how Kenny, who was just two weeks shy of his 5th birthday, slipped into the backyard above ground pool. The pool had been installed just 2 days prior. His mom found him there and called for an ambulance, but it was too late. I couldn't fight the tears as I listened to his story of a beautiful young boy that was full of life, and so quickly had it taken away. I also couldn't help thinking about the fact that I had been swimming in that pool for a couple of years and never knew that such a tragic event had occurred there.

"My parents thought about moving, but since this house was given to them by my mom's grandmother, they felt like they should stay and finish fixing it up before they sold it. Once it was all renovated, it didn't really resemble a funeral home anymore. Now, no one else in town could afford it. So they decided to stay here and try to put the accident behind them," he continued.

Gabe filled me in on all the details. Including why the room at the top of the stairs remained locked. That was Kenny's room. It was left exactly as it was on the day that he died. Now years later it remains untouched. "Sometimes I hear my mom in there, talking to Kenny." Gabe whispered. "She never really got over his death and still goes into his room to check and see if he is there, or if there are any signs of his return. He will forever remain four years old to her, and she longs to care for him again." I guess Gabe's mom didn't understand death either.

GHOST STORIES

After a couple of hours, hiding in Gabe's room, our stomachs started to growl. We slipped downstairs among the partygoers and wrestled up some fried chicken and mashed potatoes. There were several relatives there that I hadn't seen in a long time, so grandmother pulled me in to their conversation to show me off.

I had changed quite a bit since they last saw me; at least I would like to think so. I have always been a little chunky, go figure when I have to eat everything fried or pickled every summer, but I was tall, too. This year with all the walking around Halls, I started to thin out just a little. Being amongst southerners, with their big appetites and even bigger waistlines, I was feeling like I didn't blend in as much this year.

My insecurities were far away when I was on my, "summer vacation from reality." Whenever I got back to Arizona, I was reminded that everyone there was skinny, tan, and pretty, which brought me back down to reality in a snap. This year I wasn't as preoccupied by my pear shape, as Gabe and his house had become my new distraction.

I managed to abandon my grandmother's grip and met back up with Gabe who was leaning on the side of an old building in the corner of his yard. It looked like a small garage, but the weeds had overtaken the entranceway. Being my curious self, I started probing.

"Hey Gabe, what's in this garage?" I asked playfully.

"I have no idea; snakes I guess." He laughed.

I started pulling on some of the tall weeds and was surprised that they came out of the ground with ease. Gabe looked at me and looked back at the party as if he were unsure that we were supposed to be over there. When he felt the coast was clear he started pulling weeds with me. Neither of us thought about the fact that we had our nice clothes on. This seemed to be a good distraction for Gabe, I saw him crack a smile as the anticipation built. We started throwing out ideas about what might be inside.

"It's a '57 Chevy!" I suggested.

"I'll bet it's empty!" he laughingly replied.

When we finally cleared the way enough to open the door we stopped and caught our breaths. I took one side of the double door, he took the other, and we pulled it open with all of our might. The rusty hinges fought back, but we won. A puff of dust was released and got in our eyes and our noses. I wiped my face on my shirt and looked inside. Whatever it was, it was big. There were boxes piled on top of what was obviously a vehicle. I didn't recognize the front end so I wasn't sure what type of vehicle it was. It took up every square inch of the garage. There was just enough room to squeeze through the left side to get to the back. We threw the boxes out of the garage and started checking it out. It was black, but the sheen was covered in years of dust layers. The windows were long. I thought it might be a limousine, though I had only seen one in pictures.

"What is this?" I asked. "Have you ever seen a car like this? It's huge!" I walked around the side and noticed that there were black curtains in the windows. They were drawn except for a crack. "What kind of car has curtains in the windows?" I used my sleeve to wipe a spot of the window clean so I could peek inside. I couldn't see anything so I decided to get a closer look. I went to the back and saw that there was a long silver handle to open the back door. I had to clear some boxes and debris to get into a position to open the door. Gabe was on the other side but the car was so huge I couldn't see him.

"Samantha, I think I know what this is." His voice was muffled in the stuffy garage.

"It's a limousine, isn't it?" I thought we had just made an awesome discovery.

"This was a funeral home, you know. I think it's a hearse!" Gabe shouted.

"What?" I let go of the handle instantly.

Gabe met me by the back of the car and we both just looked at it. I knew that these cars existed, but I never saw one, not even a real picture of one, just a sketch in my social studies book. All I knew is that they carried the bodies from the funeral home to the cemetery. Dead bodies had been in there!

As we stood together looking at this sinister vehicle, not sure if we should run out of the garage screaming or take a peak and see what it looked like on the inside, the silence became too much.

"Should we look inside?" I asked, hoping he would say no.

"I guess so," he replied.

"Ok, you open it." He nodded and gripped the handle. All that was going through my mind was that the minute the door would open a dead body would pop out. Maybe a body was forgotten inside, just like this car was forgotten inside of the garage. My heart started to pound in my ears as he yanked on the back door. He slowly opened it and we peeked in.

Suddenly there was a rustling sound coming from within. I looked at Gabe, he looked at me, and we both went pale. Before we had a chance to fight our way back out of the pile of old boxes something flew out of the car. We both screamed and ran, leaving the door wide open. I swore the curtains moved when we ran past the side.

"Oh no, we released some spirit that was trapped inside!" I yelled as we continued running through the yard. By the time we reached the party, I noticed Gabe was laughing. I was so panic-stricken I was out of breath and here he is laughing!

"What the heck is so funny?" I asked.

"Samantha it was just a packrat. They dig into old cars all the time. We must have frightened it and it jumped out." He was out of breath from laughing and pointed at me as if I had just done something hilarious. I was mad at first then realized how silly I must have looked. All of this spooky business at Gabe's house was starting to get to me. I don't think he knew just how genuinely scared and confused I was about anything related to death and ghosts, but I gave in and laughed right along with him.

We cleaned ourselves up a bit then walked around the party again. Later, we met up out front on his porch steps. He decided that he had more stories about Kenny that he wanted to share with me, but didn't want to talk about it in his house. With all these creepy experiences, my curiosity had peaked to an immeasurable level. I wanted to know about Kenny. I wanted to know how Gabe dealt with everything. Living in this house, he was constantly surrounded by death so to me he was probably an expert. I just knew that the questions I had about death and ghosts could be answered if Gabe would share what he knew. Who would've thought that this goofy little thirteen year old would be the one that could put my mind at ease about all of this once and for all. Maybe he would even hold the key to ending my relentless nightmares about death!

Gabe began the conversation with a simple question that I didn't know how to answer. "Do you believe in ghosts? I mean real ghosts that haunt people and houses."

"Well, I don't know. Should I?" I replied trying to push away the flashbacks of the packrat that I thought was an evil spirit. He tensed up a bit when he noticed my eyes practically bulging out of my head with anticipation over what he would say next. It quickly occurred to me that this was probably the first time he had ever spoken aloud and candidly about his experiences; I should probably act less zealous.

"Well . . ." he began. "Sometimes at night I hear noises. These aren't just house settling noises, as my mom likes to say. These are noises that seem purposeful, as if someone is trying to get my attention. I feel like I am being drawn somewhere . . . well actually I feel like I'm being drawn toward Kenny's room, by some powerful unseen force. The weird thing is that I'm never scared when this happens. I'm more confused and trying to wake up from what seems like a dream. But, every time this happens, and as soon as I get to Kenny's door, I feel a jolt of electricity through my body. It's as if someone is knocking me down to the floor with a bolt of lightning. I try to wake myself up and run away, but I feel like I'm paralyzed and I can't move or yell or anything!"

As I listened, the goose bumps that covered my body felt like chicken-pocks. "How many times has this happened, Gabe?" I asked, careful not to show my true horror.

"It seems like it happens almost every night, and it's been going on since I was like eleven years old," he answered, watching for my reaction. Realizing that it has been happening for several years, I was shocked, to say the least.

"Have you ever told your mom about this?" I responded. Neither of us had really noticed this, but sometime during the conversation we started walking away from his house.

He abruptly stopped and looked at me straight in the eyes and said, "No! And don't you tell anyone either. This isn't some silly game, it's real and it's happening to me every night!"

There was a long silence as I felt his tension slowly release and he continued talking. "Every time this happens, I can almost hear my mom's voice coming from inside Kenny's room. I convinced myself that it was all just a horrible reoccurring nightmare, up until you started asking me questions. Since we started poking around the house and finding caskets and a hearse, I feel like that's all I ever think about. Now I'm so aware of what's going on in my house that memories are surfacing that I didn't even know I had; I can't figure out if they are real or dreamt." Gabe looked desperate, pale and on the brink of a breakdown.

After a little thought and a long awkward silence, I decided to play psychiatrist and try to get him to look at this event in a different way, rather than just a scary dream. I figured I had to be blunt if I was going to get to the bottom of this and really help him out. Besides, he was obviously confiding in me for a reason.

"Do you think someone or something is trying to give you a message? I saw a TV show one time where people were investigating a haunted house and asking the spirits what they wanted. Maybe someone is trying to give you a message." That sounded reasonable.

His voice quivered as he responded, "That would mean that my house is haunted, and possibly by my dead brother. That is too hard to swallow, Samantha."

GRANDMOTHER'S WISDOM

The next day I woke up wondering if Gabe had a sound sleep or was woken up in the same way, by some unknown force. I heard the creaking of my grandmother's porch rocking chair and decided to go talk to her. I don't think I've ever just sat down and had a heart-to-heart talk with my grandmother. She was one of those women who were very physically present, but seemed miles away emotionally. She constantly cooked and fussed with things, rarely sitting down to relax. I seized the moment and went down to sit on the porch swing in my pajamas, next to her.

I was searching for the right words when she looked at me and said, "I reckon you found out about Kenny. I'm sorry I haven't told you 'bout him before. It's a sore subject." My puzzled look must have given away my secret. I guess she figured that with me spending so much time at Gabe's house, that the story about

Kenny was bound to slip out. "Now you listen to me Samantha, that family has been through a lot, and the stories fly around town like a kite on a windy day. I don't want to hear folks talkin' about you going around snooping and askin' all sorts of questions. Ya just leave the answerin' to me and what I don't know, don't need to be known."

"Yes ma'am," I responded like an obedient southern child.

My questions began somewhat basic. I asked her the question that was previously posed to me, "Do you believe in ghosts, Grandmother?" She looked at me for several seconds before answering my question. I think she expected me to ask about Kenny. I would get to that later. I wanted to know what she thought. She was the wisest person I knew and her opinion meant a lot to me. I half expected her to giggle. Instead, she got very serious.

"Well Samantha, everyone has their own opinions 'bout what happens to folks when they pass. As for myself, I believe that when someone dies their spirit goes to heaven. A ghost sounds like something from a scary picture show." She stopped rocking and looked at me deep, as if she really wanted me to hear what she was about to say. She peered over the top of her glasses and raised her eyebrows as she spoke, "A spirit is not something to be afraid of."

"But they haunt people. Who wouldn't be afraid of that?" I asked. It dawned on me that she wasn't blowing me off like most adults do when you ask about something ridiculous like this. In fact, she was very serious. I broke the stare and looked away. "So then you don't believe in ghosts or spirits that haunt houses? Then what happens if a spirit doesn't get to heaven?" I wasn't sure she was going to ever answer my question, at least not the way I wanted her to answer. I wanted her to explain why some people, including myself, believe that ghosts haunt people. Her long pause gave me a chance to just start shooting questions out at her, not realizing I hadn't given her a chance to answer them: "How come only some people have experiences where they think they have seen a ghost? How can everyone go to heaven? What about the bad people?"

"Everyone gets into heaven, whether they were bad or good in life. I think that once a spirit leaves the physical body, its soul rids itself of all wrongdoing. However, I think heaven looks different to everyone. If you were the bad sort, heaven might be a place where you reconciled with the ones you've wronged. If you were good, then heaven might be a place where ya soar through the clouds and see the ones who have left before you," she explained.

I was in awe as to how closely her version of heaven matched my own. Though I liked to pretend that heaven had a room where you could watch any day of your life from the past, as a 3rd party bystander, laughing at yourself. I imagined heaven being like a movie set where I could bounce from scene to scene. I could visit a day in the life of my mom, with her bobby socks, beehive hair-do and poodle skirt as she flirted with my dad who would be leaning on his '57 Chevy convertible. I could even go back to that day in 1st grade when my mom cut my hair with a bowl and everyone teased me for a week! I think I would hide the bowl and see what happened.

My grandmother continued with her insights, "In case you're wonderin' 'bout Kenny, I do have a belief that all children have a heaven, where they live a life free of fear and loneliness. Little ones, who are as precious as Kenny was, sometimes get called to be angels sooner than we would like."

The next question I asked was one I didn't even realize I was thinking about until the words escaped my lips, "Do you think a spirit could get trapped here if the people who loved him just couldn't seem to let him go?"

"What do you mean, *let* him go?" she asked. My grandmother looked at me curiously. I had a feeling that I just put words to what she had felt herself, or maybe already knew.

"I only meant that maybe his mother can't let him go and move on with her life, that's why she hasn't changed his room, right? I wonder if maybe that keeps his spirit from being released into heaven. Does that even sound possible to you, Grandmother?"

"Well, I know Kenny's mother has never really gotten over losin' him. It's a struggle I assume most folks who have lost a baby go through. I only wish she could find some peace so she can live her life and let Gabe fill that hole Kenny left in her heart when he passed away," Grandmother said sadly. "As far as being trapped here, well, I believe spirits could use a little guidance now and again. But that can only be done by one with a strong will and a divine gift." Then she reached out, touched my shoulder, and felt this bolt of electricity shoot through my body. Before I could realize what had happened my Grandmother seemed to snap out of her serious trance and back to a relaxed position, rocking in her chair again.

"I'm sure glad you and Gabe are spendin' time together. Sometimes certain people can help those who are grieving in ways they never expected."

I wasn't sure what my grandmother was talking about. How could I help Gabe and his family? What did she mean by guidance; does someone need to tell them to "go to the light?" Was I supposed to go find a ghost buster or some eccentric woman with a crystal ball? I had a whole list of new unanswered questions now. All I knew was that if I didn't feel sorry for Gabe before, I really felt sorry for him now. I felt this sudden urge to help Gabe and get to the bottom of this situation.

INVESTIGATING

I'm not sure what happened to me that day on the porch with Grandmother, but I sure felt different. The electricity was flowing through my body and plans were hatching in my mind. I think I might be on to something. I need to find out if Kenny's mom has him trapped here, unable to go where he belongs, wherever that might be. I knew this meant facing my greatest fear of ghosts, but my grandmother's words actually gave me some strength. I kept replaying in my head when she told me that spirits were not something to fear; although that is easier said than done.

I was going to try to help Gabe escape his interrupted nights. Intuitively I believed that maybe I could help free Kenny's soul, and his mother's heart, although I had no idea how to do this. I was surprised by how confident I suddenly felt. My fears were being replaced with a real sense of purpose. This was not typical for me. Typically, if death or ghosts were anywhere near a conversation I would want to plug my ears and sing a song to drown out what was being said. Something was different about me; something was guiding me from within, like I had no control over it.

I decided to call Gabe and have him meet me at my Grandmother's house. I didn't want to risk his mother hearing our conversation. I knew that this was a tough subject for Gabe to think about and he was probably going to be really scared and emotional. Somehow I needed to make him understand what I knew in my heart was happening. I needed him to accept the fact that Kenny could be trapped in his house, haunting him and his mother.

"Hey, what's up Samantha?" he asked with an apprehensive look on his face. I had to keep reminding myself to be tender as I spoke. I was so anxious to involve myself in this puzzle.

"Hey Gabe, you want to go for a walk in the apple orchard behind Grandmother's house?" I figured that this would be a place where Gabe would feel miles away from his house and could be free to talk about things.

The orchard was a beautiful and serine place. I spent a lot of time out here with my grandfather. He loved to pick apples and trim the bushes. There were eight rows of trees: four apple, two lemon, and two grapefruit.

"How did you sleep last night?" With those simple words, tears began streaming down his cheeks. "I'm sorry; I didn't mean to upset you. I just wanted to talk to you about this whole Kenny situation." I don't think that was very tender.

"No! Last night was worse than ever. I can't even describe what I felt. Ever since you started poking your nose around and asking me questions, I started noticing more and more. This time, I decided I was going to make it inside Kenny's room, no matter what happened!" My breath was caught in my chest and I didn't move an inch as I anticipated the details. "The moment I was pulled from my bed, I began to concentrate on Kenny's doorknob. I swear I could hear my mom's voice louder than usual and clearer. She was pleading with Kenny not to go. She was crying, yelling, and begging him to stay with her. I resisted the urge to close my eyes and fought against the pain I felt in my chest. The force was unbearable, as if someone was pushing me away with iron fists. Before I could reach the door my body was frozen, like when you're trying to run in a dream but your legs don't move; I even tried to yell or scream, but nothing came out of my mouth. I woke up the next morning, in my bed with the feeling that I had been in some sort of war!" He was clutching his arms around his chest, but continued with his story. "I put my ear to Kenny's still-locked bedroom door and heard nothing but the stillness of an abandoned room. Then, I tiptoed to my mother's room and saw that she was sleeping peacefully."

"Gabe, you have to confront her about this," I meant this sincerely and not just to get answers to my questions.

"I did," he answered plainly. "She thinks I'm crazy and wants to take me to a shrink."

"She thinks you're crazy? But she's the one that talks to her dead son every night!" Again, I was not very tender. "Gabe, we have to find a way to stop this. If it truly isn't a dream . . ."

"It's not!" Gabe interrupted. "I'm telling you there is something going on in there; something that I have to stop. I just don't know how to do it. Please Samantha; you are the only one who knows. I need your help!"

His pleading was unnecessary; I wouldn't be able to just ignore such a paranormal experience. Even though the thought of going anywhere near a ghost or a haunted house scares me enough to faint, I have to see this for myself. I have always wondered about death and ghosts and now I can finally have some answers. I also felt the responsibility of helping Gabe and his family finally have peace, and help Kenny move on to wherever he is supposed to be. I somehow knew he did not belong locked in his childhood room, struggling with his mother. This newfound confidence swirled about inside of me, deep in my gut. Fear was quickly being replaced with determination.

We sat down in the orchard to hatch a plan to end this agonizing situation for good. Gabe knew all he had to do was go to bed, just like every other night; it was my role that we weren't certain of. My main objective was to get into Kenny's room and discover what was happening behind the locked door. The rest would be decided in the moment. Gabe warned me that whatever was happening in his house at night was scary and powerful. I knew that I had to be stronger and braver than ever before.

We decided that I would wait until everyone was asleep to sneak out of my grandmother's house. Gabe would lend me his bike so I didn't have to walk the two miles in the dark, getting even more terrified on the way.

No matter how hard I tried to stay calm, I couldn't swallow the lump that was stuck in my throat. When the time came, I slowly tiptoed through the house, across the creaky old wooden floor, and made my way out through the screen door. I laughed at how, just weeks prior, I would have been petrified just to do that, considering where I was headed. As I got onto the bike and started peddling as fast as my legs would take me, I glanced back at my grandmother's house. I couldn't escape the feeling that something major was about to happen, about to change my life forever.

ANSWERS

I overcame my past fears and dashed to Gabe's house, with little hesitation. It seemed like it took four seconds to reach it. The ride over was not peaceful. It was a blur of lightning bugs and the sound of my heart beating. Since Gabe had no idea what time the frightful event takes place every night, I was hoping I would have time to sneak in and take a position on the stairway that lead directly to Kenny's locked room before the excitement began.

It was cold inside the house; I shivered all the way up the stairs. Gabe was thoughtful enough to leave the door unlocked and a blanket on the top step. I tried to get comfortable on the mahogany lookout point. It wasn't until I had given in to the urge to close my eyes that it began. It took me a few seconds to get my head clear as I see Gabe practically floating across the floor in front of me. He was struggling with an invisible force, but his eyes were closed. Then I noticed the light coming from Kenny's previously darkened doorway. I had to react now, so I jumped to my feet and ran to the doorknob. Gabe was violently thrown to the floor, which jolted him awake. He began walking back to his room and abruptly stopped and swung around to face me. He reached his arms out to me but seemed to be frozen or paralyzed. I turned my attention back to the doorknob, which was ice cold. It wasn't locked but it wasn't opening either. I was so frightened yet so empowered. Some hidden instinct was now telling me that I was going to get into that room.

That's when I heard her voice. Gabe's mother sounded angry. She was pleading with Kenny telling him not to go. I pushed all of my weight onto the door and yelled, "Kenny!" Suddenly the door opened, almost as if in slow motion, and there he was; this beautiful young boy that looked like an angel, glowing with purity. His face was blurred, the light was blinding. I couldn't see, I couldn't tell what was happening. No one else was in the room so I reached my hand out towards Kenny's glow and felt a smooth warm feeling envelop me. The warmth was comforting, erasing my fear and apprehensions. I began to hear a childish giggle and the sensation of floating overwhelmed me. I heard the voices of Gabe and his mother that seemed to be getting fainter and fainter, until almost a whisper.

I realized my eyes were closed and I squinted them open unprepared for what I would see. All around me were children, beautiful and angelic like Kenny. We walked hand-in-hand through what appeared to be a colorful field, filled with laughter and sunshine. I've never felt so carefree and comfortable. I heard a woman's voice calling for Kenny behind us and we both turned to see who it was.

There before us was a woman who looked like Kenny's mother, only it was a younger version than what I knew. She had the same glow about her as everyone else in this magical place. Kenny threw his arms around her and let out a joyous yelp and said," Mommy!" She picked him up and twirled him around in her arms. She looked up, stretched her hand out toward me, and thanked me for bringing him home.

Suddenly my carefree feeling turned to confusion. The woman must have known that my cloud of bliss would quickly change to uncertainty. She encouraged Kenny to meet his "spiritual brothers and sisters" and sent him off so she could answer my questions.

"Is this heaven?" I asked, feeling I already knew the answer.

"Yes, it is," she replied.

"Who are you exactly?" I continued.

"I am Kenny's spirit guide, a version of his mother. He needs to have his mother with him to be happy, so that is what I look like to him. You can call me Alina. I am here to guide the children in their new journey. All the children you see here have crossed over and are awaiting the arrival of their family members who remain in the physical world."

"Does that mean that I too have crossed over? This doesn't look like my version of heaven. Did I die in Kenny's room?" I asked.

"You, my dear, do not belong here, this is Kenny's heaven. You are what we call a spiritual pathfinder. I have met many pathfinders on my journey. I realize that this is your first cross-over and I'm happy to help you understand, and answer all of your questions." Alina's voice was so soothing and graceful. She captivated me instantly and I listened attentively to every word she spoke.

"When you were in the physical world with Kenny you reached out to him. When you, as a Pathfinder, encounter an unsettled spirit, your spirit will take hold of theirs and find the path it was meant to travel. You helped him make the decision to leave the physical world. Your spirit guided him here, so that he could be at peace."

My ears were ringing with this new information. How could this be true? How could I, plain old Samantha, be something as important as a Pathfinder? This was the first time I started to doubt myself and wonder if I was dreaming. I looked around and realized that my surroundings had changed. We were moving swiftly, yet I didn't have the physical discomfort of running. Our quickened pace made me feel uneasy.

Just then, Alina grasped my hand and whispered, "Where are we going?"

I replied, "What do you mean?"

"You are taking us through time and space with your thoughts. When you are here you can go wherever you want, travel through time and space with a single thought. Look around and tell me where we are at," Alana's words were smiling.

"Oh, I'm controlling this travel? I was just thinking about how my heaven might look. Does that mean we are in my heaven?" I asked the question before I could figure out if it was something I would be allowed to know. Certainly there are some rules to this position. I couldn't deny what was right before my eyes. I saw my maternal grandparents, who had passed away last year. They were sitting at a round table, the one I remember from my childhood with its green vinyl top and grey metal legs; and they were playing cards. I saw my friend Sarah playing with my dog Honey, both of whom had passed away several years ago. My favorite Journey song was even playing faintly in the background.

I moved about, soaking in all of the familiar smells and sights that made me feel at peace. As I moved through the space, I remembered the room I had always hoped would be in heaven, where I could relive anytime from my past. Suddenly my surroundings changed and I was standing in the living room of my childhood home on Christmas Eve. There on the floor beside me was a younger version of myself, shaking Christmas packages and arguing with my parents about opening one early. I looked around and saw my family gathered around the dinner table, talking about the day's events. I gasped when I saw how young my father looked. My mom was in her familiar apron, fussing with dishes and trying to stay in the conversation. I marveled at my ability to be wherever I wanted to be, and was quickly transported back to the present. Alina stood beside me watching me with a heartfelt smile. I had tears of happiness running down my cheeks. "Do I get to stay here Alina?"

"It is a decision that you have to make Samantha. You have been bestowed with a gift that is needed in the physical world. Pathfinders are a vital part of crossing-over. There are many unsettled spirits that are trapped, waiting for someone like you to help them find their peace. Without Pathfinders, they are cursed to wander, often reliving the final moments of their life, and affect those in their physical world."

At that moment, I realized that I had received the answer to the question that has plagued me for so long. The "ghosts" that people talk about and are scared of, are spirits of people like Kenny, who have wandered off their chosen path. They need me!

"Will I be able to return someday, to my heaven?" I asked Alina. "Of course sweetheart, but now is not your time." My decision was made.

WARNING

Alina grasped my hand with her warmth and began to lead me through what appeared to be a gallery. It was like a hall of windows where I could see people and worlds that varied in color, scenery and population. I assumed that this was Alina's way of showing me what types of things I could expect as a Pathfinder. I was grateful for the guidance.

One window was very dark and filled with hundreds of people. I could see that it was not a happy place like Kenny's or mine. I stopped and looked at it closely, mesmerized by what was happening inside. There was a light in the background and it was the size of a pinhole. It was getting gradually bigger as the sobbing man inside began hugging and apologizing to the people surrounding him. The light began to reveal a distant land that looked happy and enchanting. But it was very far away.

My thoughts were interrupted by Alina. "There is one thing that I need you to understand. The power of an unsettled spirit varies greatly. Some spirits can have a powerful hold on their pathfinder, feeling that they need them for longer than is necessary. You can easily be trapped in their journey. This is especially true for the spirits who are not immediately at peace.

"Do you mean someone that was bad during their life and needs to make peace with others first, like the man in this window?" I was remembering my grandmother's words about bad people having to reconcile with those they have wronged, and starting to wonder how she could be so right in her beliefs about the after-life.

"Yes, and spirits who have roamed the living world for centuries can also be resistant to you. They can even be compelling to you and you will be the one to feel you cannot leave them. They often have not decided where they should be," Alina warned. "If you allow yourself to stay for too long, whether it is from curiosity or pity or even pleasure, you will start to forget about the physical world. You need to stay strong and focused and not allow these things to happen."

"Does this happen to a lot of Pathfinders?" I asked.

"Some of the younger ones lose their path. But it is not common," she said this in a way that seemed like a warning. If there is anything I know about myself for sure, it is that I can be curious to a fault. I was a bit concerned that my curiosity could get me lost forever and knew I would need to find ways to prepare myself for this. When I was helping Kenny, I was able to be stronger and braver than ever before, this gave me some comfort.

"How will I know if I am needed to cross someone over?" I asked, realizing that this was real and this was serious. "How do I find them?"

"Just as you were drawn to Kenny, you will also be drawn to other places; places where there are unsettled spirits pulling you toward them with their energy. Now that you are aware of your gift, you will notice things in a way that you never thought of before. You will listen to people and hear things that were inaudible to you before today. There are also many other Pathfinders out there that you will find," Alina explained.

This was the best news I had gotten. "How can I find them, or will they find me?" Alina giggled and touched my shoulders turning me toward a mirror that had suddenly replaced a window that was behind me. I saw my reflection and gasped. "I'm . . . glowing! I look like an angel, like you! Can everyone see this?"

"No, only other Pathfinders will see your glow, as you will see theirs. You might be surprised to see that you already know a Pathfinder; One that no longer crosses people over. See, there will come a point in your life where you do not have the strength to be a pathfinder because your journey in the physical world is almost over and the urge to stay in the after-world is too great. Many people who have lived a long life and are preparing to cross-over naturally will 'retire' so to speak," Alina winked as she said this.

My grandmother's face flashed before my eyes, and at that moment, I knew who Alina was talking about. I was sure she was talking about my grandmother. The knowledge of this tickled me. I was so surprised and relieved at the same time.

All of this information was spinning in my head and I was afraid I would forget something important. I also felt like my life had a new meaning. I was empowered with this ability and was ready to use my gifts to help people come to this magical place. I just knew that I had an important purpose and assured Alina that I would not allow myself to lose my way. I promised myself I would be strong and focused and never forget the rules.

She must have recognized my acceptance and began speaking to me in a stronger, more authoritative voice. "Now go back Samantha, use your thoughts to get you back to your physical self and begin your journey as a Spiritual Pathfinder."

I closed my eyes and felt like the wind was whipping me around, as if I was in a twister. It took so much strength and concentration. I just kept telling myself, "go back, go back, go back!" I pictured in my mind where I was when I left and the memory seemed to be light-years away. I remembered Tennessee, then Grandmother's house, then Gabe's house, then Kenny's room, then blackness. All I could see was blackness. I was starting to get scared. Had I done something wrong? Was I already lost? Then in the distant background, I could hear voices. They were getting louder, coming closer. It was Gabe and his mom. They were calling my name. I used all of my strength to open my eyes and saw their faces plastered with concern. I looked beyond their faces and realized I was on the floor, in an unfamiliar room. It was Kenny's room.

"Samantha, are you ok? What are you doing in here? What happened?" This was Gabe asking me these questions. Didn't he remember our plan to help Kenny? Is he acting in front of his mom?

"Yeah, I'm fine," I muttered.

Gabe's mom must have realized I was fine and began also asking me why I was in Kenny's room. It hit me like a ton of bricks; they have no recollection of what happened. They don't remember any of it. I could tell by Gabe's expression that he did not recall the events of the night. I began to get up and they stepped back. I had to think of something quick, a way to explain my presence here, in Kenny's room.

"Um, Gabe and I were messing around and I fell asleep at your house. Then I had a nightmare and thought it was real, I'm so sorry for waking you up." That was the best explanation I could think of. I need to come up with a better cover-up story if waking up on someone's floor is going to be a regular event in my life. "If it's ok I would like to go home now. I feel fine, really."

My aunt drove me back to my Grandmother's house, not speaking a word, and dropped me off. I was thankful that she didn't come inside, seeing as how it was still dark out and no one knew I was gone. I was sure my aunt would really think I was peculiar now and ban me from seeing Gabe. I waved to her and she drove away. I decided not to go straight to bed; I needed some time to think. I sat on the porch swing and swayed to the sound of the crickets.

Sitting there thinking, I began to piece together the events of the night. I started to wonder if it was all a dream. I had the unrelenting feeling that I was not supposed to doubt myself, but away from the magical land of heaven, it all seemed like it could have just been a dream. It had to be a dream. There is no way that I, plain old Samantha, had just gone where few mortals have ever journeyed. Could it be possible that I just visited heaven, the mysterious place that you can only read about in the bible? It made more sense to consider this all some sort of hallucination, brought about by the fresh farm air or something.

The disappointment crushed me as I talked myself into believing it had all been a dream, and I began to cry. I needed this to be true. I so badly wanted to be a Pathfinder and have a purpose in my life. Now, sitting here in on an old wooden porch swing, I was afraid it all sounded silly. I began shaking, almost in convulsions, realizing that I was just a fool. It was all just a nightmare that ended with me somehow lying on Kenny's floor. What an idiot I am to think I could be so important, so special as to have a gift that millions of people would die for!

Through my sobs, I heard a noise coming from inside the house. Great, now I was going to be caught out here. Not only am I experiencing the biggest disappointment of my life, but now I was going to get a lashing from my grandmother for being out so late. As the door slowly opened up my grandmother appeared, and she was glowing.

THE AFTERMATH

Grandmother and I must have sat on the porch for hours. The sun was slowly rising as she sat and told me about some of her adventures when she was a young pathfinder. I learned of her most emotional crossover, when she found her niece leaning over her bed one night.

Somehow, her niece, who had passed away from the flu as a young girl, found her way to Grandmothers house. She had lived in the house across the street when she died and grandmother never even knew she was haunting there. "I used to see a mysterious light in the house over yonder, but never really took the time to investigate. Then one day it was as if she appeared out of nowhere, after 10 years." Tears began forming in the corners of her eyes as she spoke of how hard it was to come back to the physical world once she crossed over her niece. I guess when it's close family like that, the things and people who you miss are in the same circles and you are bound to run in to them in heaven.

That night on the porch we laughed, we cried, we hugged, and we grew closer than I ever knew was possible. We had a connection at that moment; one that no one else would ever understand. She was my spirit guide, and I felt in my heart that she would be the one person who I could always count on for guidance and understanding.

I must have slept for two days. When I awoke, it was dusk and the house was quiet. Starved, I forced myself out of bed and shuffled to the kitchen. I could always count on my grandmother to be prepared for my hunger. She had already set out a place at the table for me and left biscuits and gravy in a pot on the stove. For the first time, I noticed a framed needlework picture that hung in the kitchen, next to the back door. It was the most powerful and poignant message that seemed to be screaming my name. It looked as if it had a red light shining on it, faint but visible. I never saw the red light before. It read:

Today your journey begins. Your life is forever changed as you have been graced with heaven's considerate gift. Now you must trust yourself to find those who will follow you to their destiny. Seek others who can comfort you and leave those who confine you. You are a chosen one and this is your calling.

My head started to spin in wonderment. This was like a message sent to me from heaven. It may have been originally intended for my grandmother, but now it was mine; all mine. I wanted to run outside and search every corner for anyone who might need me. If only I had a super-hero suit. That's how I felt; like a superhero, ready to save the spirits of the world. Reality struck and the thought of seeking out ghosts became quite terrifying. I wished I could find other Pathfinders so I could ask them the millions of questions I had swirling about in my head. My grandmother must have been at her regular Bingo night meeting so I was alone with my thoughts for a while.

I finally decided to step outside and began to wander. It was unusual for me to walk alone at night, but I had a renewed sense of strength. The darkness was falling and I found myself following mysterious glows. I was searching around, investigating anything that was brighter than a lightning bug. There were several porch lights. Then the sign from the "Soap and Suds" threw me off a bit. So, I decided to take a detour from my voyage and head over to Gabe's house. I wasn't sure whether I should go in or not, so I decided to sneak around outside and listen to the sounds of their house.

I saw Gabe's mom immediately, she was sitting on the patio. She was not alone, Gabe was sitting next to her on the bench and they were talking and laughing. I was filled with joy and pride when I saw how the forgotten events of that fateful night had altered their relationship so dramatically. They looked content, so I knew it was time I moved on. Gabe and I would talk about it someday, I was sure.

I was quickly distracted by a noise that seemed to come from the trees beyond Gabe's yard. It was faint, but I think it was a child's voice. No one on the patio was aware of the sounds, so I assumed it was meant for me. I could remember Alina telling me I would be more acutely aware of sounds that were previously inaudible to me.

I started out to follow this sound. As I approached the edge of the woods, I could see a little girl. She had red flowing hair and a white dress on, with a little pink bow around the waist. The dress reminded me of something my mother used to make me wear to church on Easter Sunday. It looked like she was skipping along with someone, though the "someone" was invisible. The little girl seemed joyous and happy, not at all what I expected to encounter. The glow that surrounded her was angelic and made her appear to be like an apparition.

Again, I had to ignore the chills that were creeping up my spine. This was definitely a ghost; a spirit as I now knew I should call it. I suddenly became aware that I was in the dark woods alone with a spirit. As sad as I was that it was of another child, she was obviously harmless and the chills began to fade. I watched the events unfold before me but wasn't sure what to do just yet.

There was a small clearing up ahead and the little girl turned toward the invisible stranger and must have challenged it to a race. The girl was laughing and carrying on, running with intent. Then suddenly she disappeared. However, I could still hear her voice. I ran to the spot where she disappeared. There was nothing, no sign of a hole or a girl. Even her glow had disappeared into the dirt. Her voice was distant and sounded like an echo. She was screaming and yelling for help. All I could make out was, "Sarah, help me!" I just knew she was in the ground somewhere, deep in the earth.

There was no one else in the woods except me and this spirit so I began digging with my hands into the hardened dirt. I felt the need to reach this young girl. I yelled toward the dirt that I was here and I was going to help her, but there was no response, just silence. The urge to continue digging overwhelmed my bloodying fingers. I dug and dug, and didn't find anything. There were no bones, no glowing girl, nothing. I had failed. The ground had swallowed her up, again. I felt awful. My first encounter since my official assignment and I lost her. I knew this was too hard for me. I needed to talk to Grandmother.

SAVING JANE

By the time I returned, my grandparents were home. Grandmother saw my disheveled state and quietly instructed me to clean up and then meet her outside. It dawned on me that her gift might still be a secret, even to her husband of 50 years. I remembered Grandmother telling me that no one can know of this gift. Others wouldn't understand because they couldn't see what we saw or hear what we heard. She even told me of an old Pathfinder she heard stories about that was locked up in a psychiatric ward because he tried to convince people of his gift. It drove him crazy that no one would believe him. It was to remain a secret, no matter what.

It took me several minutes of scrubbing to remove the dirt from my fingernails: I cried as I scrubbed. The whole time I showered, I thought about the little girl. I wondered what her name was, how old she was, where she had lived, how long she had been wandering, and why no one else had ever seen what I saw. I put my clothes on and hurried outside.

Grandmother came outside and asked me to go for a walk with her. We only went a few feet from the house when I blurted out what had happened. She pleaded with me to keep my voice down. "Oh my, that poor girl, you will have to go back and help her."

"But I was too late. How will I help her? I'm scared Grandmother; this is too hard for me! Can't you go there with me?"

"Samantha, you have to remember that the power within you is enough to end this little girl's sufferin'. If you let fear get in your way the poor soul will wander forever, relivin' the events that led to her demise. Sometimes when bad things happen, the unsettled spirit doesn't know what to do except replay the final moments of their life. You just need to get to her before she disappears into the hole. Try to make contact with her Samantha, and guide her to her destiny."

"What do you mean, contact? Can I talk to her Grandmother?" Her response surprised me. "You already know what happens when you make physical contact with the spirit. You will find that many unsettled spirits don't realize that they are no longer livin'. Yet some have been wanderin' for so long that they've gone and figured it out already. Those are the spirits who haunt others, desperately seekin' help and acknowledgement."

I knew what I had to do, but it would have to wait until tomorrow. Apparently when the spirits are in this type of loop they relive the moments of their passing at the time of their passing, every day. This time when I went into the woods I would be better prepared.

In my mind, I could imagine the scene. I decided that I would try to speak to the little girl, at least try calling to her to see if I could distract her from her pattern.

The next day dragged on so slow that I couldn't stand it anymore. I decided to go to the library and search for some answers about what had to be a tragic death of a young child. There would certainly be some news about this in the local paper.

Going to the library was not something I did too often. I had to ask for help when using the dusty microfiche machine. I had no idea how to find information about the death of a little girl in the middle of the woods. Luckily, the librarian was a fountain of knowledge. She was an older woman with bright pink lipstick, most of it stuck to her front dentures. I had a hard time focusing on her words, as I was mesmerized by her grey eyes. They looked so old and worn, yet she was very intense. She knew exactly where the renovated funeral home was; therefore, she knew the woods behind the house. She fiddled around with some microfiche film canisters and put them in the machine for me. She gave me a quick lesson on the search knob and left me alone to find the newspaper article that she said I would find in April of 1958.

The story was on the front page: "Perkins Family Tragedy." I was shocked to read that the little girl was 7-year-old Jane Perkins, the daughter of Joseph and Anna Perkins. Apparently, Jane had been last known to be playing at her friend's house after church one evening. No one knew what happened after that, but it seems that she just disappeared. There was a search for months in an attempt to find her. Locals were speculating that she was kidnapped by a young man that was arrested two counties over for kidnapping just weeks after her disappearance. No evidence of her was ever found. Joseph and Anna were both devastated. There was a picture with the article of Jane and her parents. The description of her red hair was unmistakable; this was the girl in the woods.

The last story I read about little Jane was in June of 1958, when they finally called off the search. Jane's friend, who she was playing with that day, was only five years old. The only clues she could relay were that she disappeared into the ground. That didn't make sense to anyone except me. I saw her disappear into the ground.

This newly acquired information was my driving force. I needed to help Jane get out of the ground and put a stop to her suffering. She must not realize she has passed and just replays that last moments of her death over and over again. Tears began to well up in my eyes at the thought of this. I had to help her and guide her into her heaven. She wasn't going to have to relive this horrible nightmare for one more night!

"Did you find what you needed, dear?" the librarian startled me out of my trance. "Yes ma'am thank you for your help." With one eyebrow raised she asked, "What on earth made you want to dig up this old information, dear?" This I knew how to answer, "I am doing some family research this summer, and I heard the story of Jane while interviewing family members." I was getting good at these little white lies.

The next night, my grandmother gave me a wink as I put on my jacket, readying to leave. Her casualness put me at ease. As I walked toward the woods, I saw a familiar figure headed my way on a bicycle. It was Gabe! I hadn't talked to him since the night I crossed Kenny over. I wasn't sure what to say to him or how to explain what happened. I decided, though it was difficult, that I would keep my mouth shut and just let Gabe do the talking.

"Samantha, where have you been? I have great news! Do you remember how we talked about my reoccurring nightmare? Well, it's been 3 days and I haven't had it once! And, my mom asked me if I would help her pack up all of Kenny's things so we can make his old room into a family game room! Of course, we'll leave up his pictures and some of his favorite toys to honor him. Mom thinks it's time we start acting more like a family. Isn't that great?" Gabe's excitement was contagious. I was so happy for him that I almost forgot where I was headed.

"That's great Gabe. I'm so glad you are all at peace now." I wanted to ask him what he remembered about the night that he asked me to help him. Did he remember the blanket, the bicycle, the hours of talking about Kenny?

"I wanted to thank you for helping me Samantha. Without you I wouldn't have faced my fears and stopped this nightmare." I didn't mind that he was unaware of my true role. I was actually relieved that he didn't ask me any questions.

As my mind wandered away from Gabe's compliments, so did my eyes. I saw in the distance the first signs of darkness; lightning bugs. I realized I would have to find an excuse to leave Gabe, and that would not be easy.

"Grandmother is making me go visit Aunt Winifred tonight, so I have to get going." Although I was getting better at lying, I didn't like it at all. "I can give you a ride on the handlebars," Gabe replied. "Oh thanks Gabe, but I want to walk. Besides, you don't want to get sucked in to the long and boring conversation with Aunt Winifred. I'll come by tomorrow and we can hang out."

I started walking away with intent, making it clear that I didn't want to talk any longer, but didn't realize that I was headed the wrong direction until I was a couple of blocks away. I looked back and noticed that Gabe was gone. I quickened my pace, and then broke out in a run. I felt like I was in the race for my life. My mind flickered with pictures of Jane and her parents, and the scene I was coming closer to. When I reached the woods, I instinctively hid, as if I could affect the occurrence.

I'm not sure how long I waited there in the woods, but it seemed like a lifetime. I was about to give up and leave, when suddenly I heard the giggle. I was closer than before so I just listened for a minute. This time I heard the words she was saying, "Want to race Sarah? I bet you can't catch me!" There were no audible responses. I had to pull myself together and make my move.

I stepped out from behind the tree and shouted, "Jane, come here I want to race with you." She stopped and turned around. She was looking right at me but it looked as if she was still being pulled away, headed for the spot where she disappeared. "Come here Jane, my name is Samantha and I'm your friend." She struggled to pull away from the force but seemed to be stuck in the forward motion. I ran to her and she started screaming. She looked scared but I kept going. I had to get to her before she disappeared into the hole again. "Jane, give me your hand. I can help you!"

She looked at me intensely, and said, "I have to go down to the water." Then like a movie that had been on pause, she went right back to her routine. I knew what was coming so I leapt forward and grabbed for her.

The minute I felt her warmth we were transported. In the whirl of the journey, I looked at Jane. She was more beautiful and angelic than even Kenny was. She gripped my hand tightly and closed her eyes as if on a roller coaster ride. She asked me where we were going; but before I had a chance to answer, we were there.

Jane's heaven was very unusual compared to what I had seen before. We were in what appeared to be a backyard. There were tons of people there. Jane looked up at me with her big green eyes and mouthed, "I'm home."

I took a moment to look around and noticed her parents running toward her with open arms. I knew it was time for me to go but being my curious self I decided to stay for a bit. It looked like there was a party going on. I think it was a "Welcome Home" party. I was tickled by the hairstyles and outfits; they were straight out of a 50's Coca-Cola commercial.

Though many people were celebrating, swimming and barbequing, there was a little girl who was standing off in the distance, with a distinctively sad look on her face. She was not glowing brightly like the others at the party. She almost seemed to be encased in a shadow. The girl was young and dressed like Jane, in a sweet little dress and Mary Jane shoes. I noticed Jane walk towards the little girl, stopping right in front of her. It only took me a moment to realize who it was. This was Sarah, the girl who must have held the guilt of not being able to help find little Jane for her entire life. There was a short pause as the girls looked at each other and finally embraced. I could see Sarah's glow become instantly brighter. They returned to the party hand-in-hand and began playing together. I was amazed at how easily it was to be forgiven in heaven, and how everyone was the age that the deceased last remembered him or her. I wondered if this was only true for children.

I decided it was time for me to go back, so I closed my eyes and pictured myself back in the spot where I left with Jane. Knowing what to expect now, I just enjoyed the floating sensation until I felt my soul reconnect with my physical body. When I came to I was on the floor in the woods, but there was something about the spot I was laying on that was different from when I had left. There was an unusual glow and warmth coming from below the surface of the earth. I began, just as I did yesterday, to dig with all my might.

Just then, I was interrupted by a voice, it was Gabe. "Samantha, what is going on? What happened just now, and why are you digging in the dirt? Why aren't you at Aunt Winifred's house?" Oh no, he must have followed me. I can't give away my secret, but my ability to lie is not that great.

"Is there a well around here that you know about Gabe?"

"There are old wells all over these parts of the woods. I guess there could be one over here. Why?"

Geez, why does he have to ask so many questions? "Well, I went to the library today and heard someone talking about a girl who disappeared about 30 years ago or so and it was right back here behind your house. I just wanted to see if it was true. Can you just help me dig so I can see if there's a well over here?" He gave me a disbelieving look, but accepted my weak explanation and started digging. It didn't take long before I spotted the little pink bow from Jane's dress and I stopped the digging immediately. I decided to let Gabe give me a ride on his handlebars to the police station to tell them what we found.

It turned out I was right about the well. I read later that week, in the local paper, that Jane was finally laid to rest with the rest of her family in the Halls Cemetery. I decided someday I would visit her there.

A FORBIDDEN FRIEND

It took a lot of energy to avoid Gabe. He followed me a lot these days. I guess he was suspicious after the night in the woods. I tried not to let it disturb me, so that I could concentrate on my task. I really wanted to find another Pathfinder to swap stories with and to learn about forgiveness in heaven. In between making wooden treasures in the garage with my grandfather, picking beans and potatoes for grandmother, and flattening pennies on the railroad track, I wandered around searching out glows.

One morning, my grandparents and I had breakfast in town. This was a pretty big deal, as we never went out to eat. I think they took me out because my time in Halls was ending soon. Summer would be over in just two short weeks. I never wanted to stay in Tennessee so bad. I was always excitedly counting down the days until I returned to civilization, to my real life. This time I was so afraid to leave, that I didn't even look at the calendar. What if when I leave Halls I leave my Pathfinder powers behind? That sounds silly, but I didn't know how this whole thing worked. I wanted to make the best of the remaining time I had here, just in case.

While we were driving home from breakfast, my grandmother suggested that we stop by an old friend of the family's house. I wasn't looking forward to hanging out with old people whose house probably smelled like mothballs. I know that their house is in a different part of town than I have ever been to and so I was curious about what I might find there. My neighborhood seemed to be glow-free.

When we arrived, a few things caught my interest. I saw an old barn across the street, a small cemetery behind that, and a dilapidated house that gave me a funny feeling in my gut.

After spending a few minutes getting to know my grandparents' friend, I asked if I could be excused to go for a walk outside. I said I wanted to "walk off my breakfast," which everyone agreed was a good idea. I wasn't outside but a few minutes when I felt the pull. It was as if someone were pulling me by my torso toward this old house. It was obviously abandoned, which is not unusual in the backwoods of Tennessee. Usually, when it was time to move out, people left their house. They just packed up, walked out the door, and left the house vacant for someone else to move in to. The house looked like a box with eaves. It was a two story house, but small and simple. The white paint had long worn away, leaving bare gray wood with rusty nail heads scattered about.

I was glad it was daytime, because it was less scary to walk in to this old house with the sun shining. I opened the front door and called in, "Hello. Is anybody home?" I didn't hear any voices but I definitely heard footsteps upstairs. The hair on my neck was standing up. It doesn't matter how brave I tell myself I am, or how focused I am, it still scares me to confront a spirit. I stepped back outside and looked around. I went to the back porch and sat down on the wooden step, trying to gather my courage. I knew there was a spirit trapped inside, but so far, I have only encountered children. What if this was a scary man?

I heard what sounded like a window creaking open. It came from a room upstairs. There were old drapes on the broken windows that were moving, even though there was no breeze. I felt like this might be an invitation to come inside. I gathered my courage and headed in through the back door this time. I entered through the kitchen, but I could see the staircase from where I was standing. Suddenly a figure walked past me and stood in the kitchen doorway. I was startled and turned around to run out the door.

"Wait! Can you help me find my musket?" I stopped at the sound of his voice; it was gentle and shaky. I slowly turned back around, but he was gone. Not again, I thought. Another missed opportunity to help someone. Then he reappeared in the doorway. It was a young man, but his glow was faint. He almost looked like he was alive, just a little faded. He was wearing odd-looking clothes. They were definitely hand made. It almost appeared as if it were an old-fashioned uniform. He stood in the threshold looking at me with pleading eyes. He was definitely handsome, so much so that I think I blushed.

"Hello, I'm Samantha. I'm sorry I don't know where your musket is." I studied his face as he studied mine. We were both confused about what we were seeing. Our eyes met and I felt a rush of emotions from my head to my toes. I had butterflies in my stomach and was at a loss for words. This must have been the most beautiful being I have ever set my eyes on. He was so innocent and naïve looking. I felt like I was looking at a lost puppy dog pleading for its home. I decided to cease the opportunity to encounter a real ghost. I know I could end his wandering with a simple touch, but my curiosity kept me at a distance.

"What's your name?" I asked the handsome stranger. "Private Jonathan Terino," he replied. He reached out to shake my hand and I swiftly dodged his advance by turning toward the window and asked more questions.

"Is this your home, Jonathan?"

"I don't think so. I mean, it isn't the house my mama raised me in. I came here after I was wounded fighting' the Yankees. They caught up with our battalion outside of Fort Pillow and I was hit in the ribs. This nice family took care of me for a long time.

I wanted to get back up and fight, but I was too weak and they didn't think I could make it. They left a long time ago and I want to get out of here. Now I'm searchin' for my musket, but I seemed to have misplaced it. Are you sure you haven't seen it?"

"I'm sorry that I haven't, did you look upstairs?" I needed some time to think about how to approach Jonathan and tell him that he is dead and the Civil War was over a long time ago. He disappeared up the stairs, still talking about his battalion and wanting to meet up with his fellow soldiers. I thought about telling him that the war was over first then getting to the dead part later. That seemed to be the best strategy.

"Jonathan, can you come down here for a minute?" the butterflies were full speed ahead in my stomach. Just saying his name was surreal. But, there was no answer. It was as if he disappeared again. It took all my might to climb up the rickety staircase without freezing in fear. I couldn't believe I was in a haunted house, not one of those fake mall Halloween gimmicks, but an actual house that was being haunted by a spirit. My curiosity won over my fear and I walked in to the bedroom at the top of the steps.

He was lying on the bed with his hand over his forehead as if checking for a fever. "Oh, I'm sorry ma'am; it's just that I'm so confused. I haven't talked to anyone in a long time. You're the first person I could ever get to answer my questions. I think I'm lost. Can you help me?" Of course, I knew I could help him, but my desire to keep him with me in the physical world was overruling my sensibility.

"How long have you been here, in this house?"

"I'm not too sure how long it's been. I just know that things have changed many times and so have the people. For a long while, there was a man sleeping in my bed and I tried to ask him to kindly leave, but he ignored me. Everyone ignored me. I would scream, yell, kick and even throw things across the room, just trying to be heard. No one even looked at me. They all just got scared and ran off. I just wanted to find my musket so I could get back to the battlefield. My company and my family must be worried sick about me." Jonathan got up and looked out the window, but I had a feeling he didn't see what I saw.

Before I had a chance to ask him to describe his surroundings, he turned around and looked at me. He got real close to my face and stared into my eyes with a suspecting gaze. "How come you can see me and hear me, but no one else could?"

"Jonathan, I need to tell you something that might be hard for you to hear." I stepped away from his angelic face and put my head down. The words weren't coming to me like I had hoped. What I was about to say to him is either going to relieve him or upset him. "I think you might have died from your wounds during the war. This was probably the last place you were at when you were alive."

"What? I don't understand. That doesn't make any sense at all. I remember being' here in this very room, being cared for and fixed up. I can't be dead, it's just not true." Though his words sounded as if he didn't believe me, I could see his facial expression fall. He didn't want to believe me and soon his expression turned angry.

"Who are you and why are you telling' me these lies?"

"Jonathan, when was the last time you ate a meal? Can you remember fixing any food, or sitting down to eat at the table?"

"Well, I couldn't eat. I was being' nursed back to health." His words carried an air of uncertainty.

"What about all those people that couldn't see you or hear you. Can you explain why that happened?"

Suddenly he plopped onto the edge of the bed and put his head in his hands. He began to sob and looked up at me with melancholy eyes. "So does that mean that I'm in heaven? This house, this bed, this is it? My mama always said that the Lord would take me to a beautiful place when I died. I studied the bible in school for a while and I don't remember readin' nothin' about an empty house."

I couldn't help but giggle to myself a bit. I wanted to tell him that he would soon be in a magical place where all of his pain and worries would disappear. He would be in heaven reuniting with his friends and loved ones. I decided to hold off just a bit more. I felt like we had a connection, something deep and intriguing. I wanted to spend more time with him. I soon realized that it was getting late and I had to decide if I would take him now or wait until I had more time to spend with him.

I chose to be selfish, which I would probably regret later. For now, Jonathan was my secret and I wanted to have him for a little bit longer. When I told him that I had to leave, he was sad and afraid. I hated to do that to him, but was unsure of how to comfort him without losing him.

"I'm sorry that I have to leave, but I will be back tomorrow, I promise." I turned to leave but he followed me down the stairs.

"How old are you?" Jonathan asked unexpectedly.

I wasn't sure why he was asking this, but I answered with a quizzical look on my face, "Fourteen. How old are . . . I mean were . . . I mean are you?"

"Well, I guess I'm still seventeen." He almost cracked a smile, though pain was still burning in his eyes. I felt incredibly guilty, but just couldn't let him go yet.

I crossed the street and turned one more time to see if he was at the window or outside watching me go. All I could see was his hand on the broken glass of the upstairs bedroom window. Suddenly, it disappeared and that made me feel anxious.

I hopped into my grandfather's car and we headed back to Halls. My grandmother turned to look at me in the back seat and her facial expression caught me off guard. She looked mad or disappointed or something. I wondered what she knew or what she suspected. I began piecing things together in my head and realized that she must have brought me to that neighborhood on purpose. Did she know that house was being haunted? If so, how could she tell that I hadn't carried through with the crossover? She didn't speak a word the whole ride, despite my bombardment of futile questions. She wouldn't even tell me what we were having for dinner.

When we arrived at my grandparents' house, my grandmother shouted to my grandfather that she and I were going to pick some beans from the garden and he should go inside and get the chicken ready. I tried not to make eye contact with her as I picked long green beans from the garden. Grandmother marched right up next to me and said, "I am very disappointed young lady. What happened in that house? Did you let your fear get in the way again? When will you learn that you have the power to overcome your fears so that you can help people? You need to make this right; it is your responsibility Samantha." I wasn't sure if I should tell her the truth or lie and ask for another chance to help Jonathan. That would at least get me another ride over to see him.

"I'm sorry Grandmother, but he kept disappearing. Then I got scared and wasn't sure what to do. Can I have another chance? Will you take me back there to see, I mean to help him?"

"Well, it isn't going to be till next Sunday, unless I can get your granddaddy to let me use the car. How am I going to explain all of this? Child, you have got to get over your fears."

"I know. I'm sorry."

"It ain't me you're hurtin' it's that poor soul." With that, she turned and walked out of the garden with barely enough beans for one.

LOST AND FOUND

Later that evening as I lay in bed I longed to comfort Jonathan. I thought about how I left him there with all of this information, and how he must be so confused right now. Of course, maybe spirits forget and start fresh every day. That can't be right, because he remembered the man sleeping in his bed. I hope that time for them isn't the same as it is in the physical world.

I thought about Jonathan all night. Even as I sat and watched TV with my grandparents, my thoughts were constantly on the striking young man I met and the prospect of seeing him again. My heart raced with excitement as I thought about his angelic presence. I started thinking of ways that I could keep him with me, putting off his crossover for as long as possible. Suddenly I fretted my departure from Tennessee.

This was definitely the most amazing thing that ever happened to me and I wanted it to last longer.

My selfish thoughts soon were replaced with pity for Jonathan. He was so confused and had been this way for many years. I couldn't help wanting him to stay, but knew I had to end his torment. He had a family that lost him and didn't know what happened to him. He was never properly united with his parents. The sorrowful feeling sank deep in my gut and I ran to my room, put my head in the pillow, and cried.

Just then, a voice came from inside my room. "Why are you crying Samantha?" I must have flown ten feet in the air. It was Jonathan. How did he find me? How did he get here? Why was he here?

"Oh, Jonathan, you frightened me. How did you get here?"

"I'm not sure. I just wanted to see you and suddenly I was here in your room." He seemed just as confused as I was. He sat in the wooden rocking chair that my grandfather made for me. He looked ironically like a saintly night light, sent to brighten up my room ever so slightly. His face was much more peaceful as we just looked at each other in wonderment. It dawned on me that he was just as intrigued by me as I was by him. The words, "I just wanted to see you," rang in my ears like a melodic lullaby. We seemed to stare at each other for several minutes until a knock at the door broke our gaze.

"Samantha, we're going to bed. Turn off that light soon and hit the hay." Luckily, it was my grandfather, as my grandmother would have further investigated the glow.

I gathered my thoughts and turned back to Jonathan only to find him examining my room. I bet he felt like an alien here. My room had two posters: one was of my favorite actor and one was of my favorite band. There was also a pin board of pictures of my family and friends back home. They let me hang this stuff so I didn't feel homesick in the summertime. Jonathan's attention turned back to me and I flinched, catching myself in a deep stare fixed right on him.

"I want to know if you can answer some questions that I have. Since you told me that I'm . . . well . . . deceased, I guess I'm not sure what else to do. I hope I'm not imposing on you."

"Of course not, I'm so happy to see you. And you can ask me anything you'd like."

"Well, first of all, has the war ended?"

"Yes Jonathan, the Civil War has been over for about 120 years or so, and people of all colors are free and equal." In my mind, he was fighting on the wrong side of the battle, so I said that with a genuine smile on my face. He just sort of looked at me and shrugged his shoulders, like he had just realized that none of that mattered anymore anyway. He had more important things to think about.

At that point, I began rambling on about all the things that had happened in the past hundred years, including indoor plumbing, which he thought was despicable. I showed him my headphones, and he tried to find the people inside the tape player. Then he looked around the room, touched everything, played with the light switch, and jumped on the bed. It was like watching a little kid in a toy store, not knowing what to play with first. In that moment I felt like he was mine and no one else could ever take him away from me. I wondered how long he would stay. Someday he would realize that his parents were one single touch away, and my hold on him would be gone.

We looked through my old toy box and he marveled at all of the gadgets and gizmos that had been invented. His favorite was the television, of course. I had a small black and white one in my room and I turned it on but kept the volume real low so my grandparents wouldn't hear it. He was just in awe. I loved to watch him play with everything and touch everything. We had so much fun. Every so often, he would stop and look at me with a wide smile and that beautiful glow. I didn't want the night to end.

I was getting tired and the stress of making sure we never had physical contact was wearing on me. I decided to ask him to leave until tomorrow so that my grandmother didn't find out, but to guarantee that I would see him again. I hoped that we didn't get to borrow the car in the morning, which would end my bizarre imaginary courtship much too soon.

I must have fallen asleep right away, because when I woke up the rocking chair was empty and I don't remember how I left off with Jonathan. Was he coming back tonight? Was I supposed to meet him somewhere?

I couldn't remember. I wondered if he were back at the house, no longer searching for his lost musket, I'd assume.

I spent most of the day wandering around the garden and helping my grandfather make his famous "Tater Bins," his trademark Christmas/Birthday/Wedding gift. Who knew there was such a need for a wooden bin to hold potatoes? The construction helped keep my mind slightly occupied, until Gabe stopped by.

"Hey Samantha, you want to go for a ride with me? My mom said I could let you use my bike and I could use my dad's bike. I kind of wanted to check out the new bait shop in town."

Of course, my mind started racing and calculating. Could I find a way to convince Gabe to ride over to Jonathan's house? Usually Gabe did whatever I wanted to do, since he was bored most of the time. My visits to Tennessee were usually the highlight of his summer.

"Sure. Is that okay with you Granddaddy?"

"I don't mind, but you kids need to be back before dark, or yer grandmother will have my hide!"

We set off toward town, but where we needed to go was about 4 miles past the new bait shop. I thought about just ditching him, avoiding any more lies. I could just imagine my aunt sending out a search party for me. Therefore, I decided to bribe him.

"Hey Gabe, I have $8.00 of my birthday money in my pocket. I'll give it to you so you can get a new fishing pole, if you let me borrow your bike for the day. But you aren't allowed to ask me where I'm going."

"But I thought we were going to hang out together. I don't want to go fishing by myself."

"Fine, I will fish with you all day tomorrow if you just say yes, and don't tell anyone about it." I was hoping he would just take the deal and let me go. It was already lunchtime and the ride would take a while.

"Samantha, you're so weird sometimes. Let me see the money first." I showed Gabe the money, and was happy it was still in my shorts from yesterday when we went to town. I handed the cash over to him and took off before he could change his mind. I knew he wouldn't follow me this time, not with the prospect of a new fishing pole in his future.

It didn't take too long to get to Jonathan's house, although I did get lost for a few minutes. Luckily, I'm one of those people with a built in compass rose in her brain. I really just need to go somewhere once and I can remember the details. You turn right at the Sinclair Gas Station and Left at the split oak tree. I went too far at first, but as I got closer to his house, I felt the pull again. This time it gave me a thrill and I let the force take me toward Jonathan.

By the time I reached the old house, the anticipation of seeing him had grown into full-blown angst. I wondered if he felt the same about seeing me. I parked the bike against the back porch steps and ran inside with excitement. As I passed through the hallway, I saw Jonathan pacing the floor above the steps.

"Samantha!" he called to me as if we had been apart for decades and were finally reuniting. I saw his arms open up, inviting an embrace, but I stayed put at the bottom of the staircase. Oh how I wanted to wrap my arms around him, too. I wanted to comfort him and put his mind at ease, so I started up the stairs. As I moved slowly from one step to the next, I looked at him in the eyes. His deep blue eyes were burning with anticipation. He saw the look of hesitation on my face and lowered his arms.

"Jonathan, the moment we touch our friendship will end."

"Why? I mean my apologies Samantha. I am just happy to see you."

"I know, but you don't understand. You can't touch me and I can't touch you." He backed away and let me climb to the top of the steps untouched. I can imagine the questions swirling about in his head. So, I felt I owed it to him to explain and let him make the decision as to whether he was ready to cross over or not. In a way, I felt this would make us even closer. I began from the beginning, telling him about Kenny and about heaven. I even told him about my heaven and the tremendous feelings of comfort that come with being in heaven. His eyes bulged when I told him that he too would be surrounded by people he loved, missed, and longed for. Then I told him that I would have to go back and would likely never see him again.

He hadn't said one word while I was babbling away. Once again, I overwhelmed him with information.

I needed to learn how to censor myself. He started pacing again and I tried to lighten up the situation by saying, "I wonder if ghosts can wear away wooden floorboard?"

He stopped and looked at me, then looked at the floor, then burst out with laughter. He realized at that moment, that I was just as curious about him as he was about me. "I bet I could," he said with a smirk.

"I bet there are a lot of things you can do that you didn't realize. You spent too much of your time looking for that darned musket." We both doubled over with laughter. He took a deep breath and said, "watch this," then disappeared in a blink of an eye.

"Where are you?" I called out.

"Down here," and he peeked his head out of the kitchen. I ran downstairs to find him, feeling like we were playing hide and seek. He wasn't there.

"I'm going to find you Jonathan, you met your hide and seek match with me!" I giggled and ran around the house, then spotted him peeking in through the window from outside. "Hey, get back here, I saw you. That means you're it!" I ran, only to be stopped by a solid figure. Startled, I looked up and saw my grandmother.

"What are you doing here grandmother?"

"I would like to ask the same of you Samantha."

"I was looking for the spirit, you know, the one from yesterday. I . . ."

"He's here I can feel his presence. Are you having trouble or making trouble?"

"I just can't catch him, that's all. Can we just go home now?"

"Let me take a look around and see if I can help. Sometimes these spirits are just afraid. He must be an old soul if he has figured out how to avoid you." She walked into the kitchen as if she owned the place. She went upstairs and through the rooms, one by one. I was hoping and praying that Jonathan would stay hidden. He knew that he could cross over at any time, but I so wanted him to stay with me longer. We have so much we could learn from each other, if he was willing to stay.

Just then, I saw him peek his head around the corner of the house. He put his finger to his lips as if to say, "shhh, don't let her find me."

"Maybe he's just not ready Grandmother. Can't I wait and come back another time? Please!" I was trying not to giggle and let her in on our game. I whispered to him to visit me tonight and he agreed, and then disappeared again.

We loaded Gabe's bike into the trunk, but had to keep it open since it didn't fit in the old car. I felt ashamed as I sat next to Grandmother on the ride home. Jonathan was a big secret, and I felt like I should tell her all about him. My fear of losing him was too strong. Instead, I asked her questions that I hoped wouldn't make her too suspicious.

"Have you ever talked to any of the spirits that you helped?"

"Oh yes, several times actually. However, I soon found out that the less they know the better off they are. It seems to me that most of 'em are so confused that the only thing that can really help them is to be immediately crossed over. Now I know many of 'em don't trust physical beings, because when they needed help no one would pay any attention to 'em. If you start talkin' to some of the older souls they might be afraid to go to heaven."

"But what if they chose to stay here; like if they realized they were dead and just accepted it. Could they go and do whatever they wanted here on earth?"

"I suppose so. But it's our job as Pathfinders not to let that happen, Samantha."

I was happy to see that we were home. I didn't want to hear anymore. I wanted to get back to feeling excited and anxious to see Jonathan again.

GOODBYE FOR NOW

Nighttime couldn't come any sooner. When it was time for bed, I went into my room and locked the door. I sat by the window, half expecting to see Jonathan walking down the street.

"Boo!" He startled me right out of my slippers.

"Geez Jonathan, you can't do that to me. You are a ghost ya know!" We laughed and it was as if we were back in our own little world. He immediately started going through a mental list of questions that he must have saved up for me. He asked about the big machines in the sky, which were airplanes. Then he asked about the machine that carried me home, which was a car.

"Okay, it's my turn to ask the questions, you've hogged this conversation for too long." He stopped looking out the window and sat on the rocking chair again. "What was your life like in the 1800's? Did you have any siblings or friends? Did you have a girlfriend?"

"I guess my life was fairly plain compared to yours. I helped my daddy on the farm and my mama with the children. Oh, I had one brother and two sisters. They were all younger than I was which kept me busy. My parents were very nice, but my mama got sick a lot. She was just devastated when my dad sent me off to fight in the war. I guess I miss my baby sister the most though. She was so cute, and thought I was her daddy since I was always taken' care of her. Her name was Claire.

My brother, Zacharias, was the oldest of the three; he was 15 when I left. He was never too good at helping around the house though. He preferred to go down to the river, study the animals, and make dams. He even found a way to redirect some of the Mississippi into a deep pool for the kids to swim in without worrying' about being' carried off. He was a smart kid, but hated chores.

My other sister, Laura, was very funny. She acted like she was the family pet most of the time. She would make me pet her and feed her under the table. Mama hated it, but couldn't help but laugh." As Jonathan reminisced about his life, he would turn his head and laugh to himself, but by the end of the story, there were tears welling up in his eyes.

"Jonathan, do you want me to take you to see your family now?"

"It's no use, I already tried to go to where I remember my house being, but there was some big schoolhouse right where our property used to be. I sure would like to know where they are, or what their lives were like without me. I bet mama missed me something' awful. And little Claire . . ." His voice drifted off and he put his head down.

I wasn't sure if this would work, or if it would make him sadder, but I felt an obligation to him and wanted to give him some real answers about his family. I knew that once he was in his heaven his family would likely appear to be the same ages they were when he left. "What I meant was that I could take you to the cemetery and we could try to find their gravestones. Sometimes you can find out how old they were when they died, and if they had any kids. Just don't try to go alone. Let me be there with you, okay?" Jonathan agreed and we made plans for the next day.

Trying to sneak around in my Grandparents house was no easy task. My grandmother definitely sensed that something was up, so she liked to fill my time with gardening chores. This time though, I wasn't alone. Jonathan showed up and I was ecstatic, but his glow made me nervous. My grandmother was just up the way in the house and she never missed a beat. I just knew she would come out to see what was going on, so I made him hide in between the isles of long corn stalks. He was dying to help me so it would be done faster, and we could leave to the cemetery quicker.

"Samantha, are you finished yet? I need those taters."

"Yes, Grandmother, I'll be right there!" I ran to drop off my spoils and ask if I could go visit Gabe. She never said no when it came to Gabe. She felt sorry for him and figured I was a good distraction for him. I promised to be back in time for supper, which was hours away.

I still had Gabe's bike so I jumped on and started down the street, toward the county's cemetery. I figured since it was the oldest and the biggest cemetery, we had a good chance of finding Jonathan's family plot here. I didn't want to tell him this, but they probably had to move the graves off the family's land when they built the schoolhouse. This is the cemetery that my great-great grandparents had been moved to when their land was "taken" as my grandfather says. I had high hopes that we would find out that his sisters lived long and happy lives, filled with children and husbands. I also envisioned his brother's gravestone showing that he was a doctor or a scientist or something. Unfortunately, not much of this would be true.

When we arrived at the Lauderdale County Cemetery, Jonathan was anxiously trying to find any gravestone with the last name of Terino on it. I calmed him down and told him to concentrate and close his eyes and transport himself there like he does when he goes to my house. Suddenly he disappeared, right before my eyes.

"Samantha, I'm over here!" His voice was distant but I could see him at the far edge of the cemetery. I set down the bike and ran over to him. When I got there I was out of breathe and excited. Jonathan was sitting on the ground looking at a small, modest stone that read, "Felicia Terino, mother and wife, 1829-1864".

"She must have died shortly after I left." His sadness tore a hole in my chest. Even though he knew she was sick, he must have hoped that his mother would recover and live a long life.

"I'm so sorry Jonathan." I didn't know what else to say to him. I wanted to wrap my arms around him tightly, but knew I couldn't. I've never wanted to touch someone so much as I did Jonathan. It was painful to keep my distance.

I tried to distract him after I noticed that there were many other Terinos in this area. Maybe we could find a happy story to focus on.

"Look, over here. Claire Terino Jasner," this must be your little sister. She got married! Her gravestone read, "Daughter, Sister, Wife and Mother, January 14th 1859-May 1st 1879." Oh no, she was only 20. This is getting worse, not better. Right next to her was a smaller gravestone that read, "Daniel Jonathan Jasner May 1st 1879-July 2nd 1885." Daniel must have been Claire's son. He was only five years old when he passed away. My heart sank and I looked up at Jonathan. His eyes were filled with anger as he started kicking the ground. He fell to his knees and punched the grass with clenched fists. Jonathan knew without question that this was his sister and she had died giving birth to a son, who she named after him.

"Why did you bring me here?" his voice was an unrecognizable tone. "I wish I never came here with you. I should have gone when I had the chance. Take me there now! Take me to see my family!"

"Wait, maybe the rest of your family was fine. Don't you want to see? I'm sorry about your mom and your sister and your nephew. I promise that you will see all of them soon. Just stay a little bit longer. Please!"

Jonathan's facial expression turned from anger to confusion as he looked past me at something that must have caught his eye. I was afraid to turn away from him, fearing he would disappear again. Then I felt someone push by me as if I was invisible. Jonathan reached for me, his eyes wide and scared. The stranger was walking full force toward Jonathan and before I had a chance to register what was happening, it was over.

UNINVITED GUEST

All I saw was the glowing back of a stranger reaching toward Jonathan, and in an instant Jonathan was gone. The stranger lay on the floor unconscious, tempting me to kick him while he was defenseless. He had taken Jonathan; crossed him over without me. I was instantly devastated. I wanted to meet his family and share in his joyous reunion. I wanted to be the one that he looked at and thanked with the deepest appreciation. Worst of all, I wanted him to stay with me longer. Jonathan was mine and some stranger just barged in and took him away, forever.

Suddenly I felt the need to find another unsettled spirit in a hurry. This time I wouldn't ask questions, I wouldn't even worry about a name. I just wanted to go, find Jonathan, and reunite with him in his heaven. Would he remember me? Would he care about me when he was surrounded by the family he longed for and missed terribly? Would I be able to find him?

Frantically, I got myself together and ran for the bike. I would search every abandoned house, every mysterious corner of Halls to find my ticket back to heaven to find my Jonathan.

Before I was halfway across the cemetery, I heard a yell. "Hey, wait! Come back! What's your name? Wait! I'm sorry, I thought you needed help!" I had no time to chitchat; I was on a mission. Although I was extremely curious about this new Pathfinder, the first one I had ever seen, besides Grandmother, I didn't care enough to stop and investigate. "Whoever you are, I come here every Monday at three-o-clock if you change your mind." The voice was distant, but I heard it. I did file that information in the back of my mind, just in case I ever decided to come back and kick his butt for taking this experience away from me.

It didn't take long for me to find a wandering spirit. In fact, I wasn't even out of the cemetery when I spotted a woman sobbing under a tree at the edge of the woods that acted as a border around the cemetery. I changed directions and headed for her. Her glow was bright and startled me a bit. I was used to Jonathan who was more like a 10 watt Christmas bulb. This woman was a flood light compared to him. I stopped thinking about it and just walked. I must have scared the woman, because she took off into the woods at the sight of me. Great, now I have to chase this woman! I knew it was insensitive of me but I really needed to get to Jonathan before he forgot about me. I could see her every move because her glow acted like a flashlight, leading me through the thick maze of trees. I was winded after a few minutes and stopped to catch my breath. The glow disappeared and I turned around to go back.

As I got closer to the cemetery, I saw her again. She was sitting in the same spot as before, but now that I was behind her, I noticed that she was wearing a white nightgown that had bloodstains all over the lower half. I wanted to know what happened to her, but was afraid it would distract me from my mission. I got real close to her and just dove. We made contact and were off. I could hear her crying and knew there was something wrong. Usually at this point, there is happiness and joy. Why was she still sad? When the transport ceased I looked around and everything was blank. It was just her and I in a blank white space, void of any color or objects. I was so confused. Where were we? Did I make a mistake?

I turned to look at the woman and saw that she was still sobbing. I looked down and noticed that the blood was gone from her gown, but there were large scars on her wrists. This was something I recognized from health class, where the teachers tell you about suicide and depression.

"Did you do that to your wrists?" I asked gently.

"Yes." Her answer was sorrowful.

"Why?"

"My husband left me and I wanted him to come back. I didn't mean for this to happen. I just wanted him to see me, to feel my pain." She put her head down and stared at the scars.

"I'm sorry that you were in so much pain. I don't know what to tell you to do to make it better. Maybe you need to forgive him, or forgive yourself. I have seen many powerful things happen here with a little forgiveness." I wondered how suddenly I just seemed to know the answers. I was right, too. She began walking around in the blank space, talking to herself. The woman began by forgiving her husband for leaving, and forgiving her friends for not being there for her when she needed help. It wasn't until she finally forgave herself that her heaven began to fill up. She was forgiving herself for hurting her parents, and for hurting her friends. It filled up with beautiful scenery and people who were happy to see her. When it was time to go the woman gave me a quick wave and I noticed her scars were gone.

For a moment, I had forgotten that my purpose for being there was to see Jonathan. I closed my eyes and imagined myself with him. I felt a breeze and the feeling of moving overwhelmed me. It was much stronger than before. As I opened my eyes I was surprised to see that I was once again back in the cemetery. I thought that maybe I was here because this is where I last saw Jonathan. Maybe I was still in heaven and his heaven looked like Halls. I was more than confused about how I got here, but I was definitely in my physical form. I knew this because I could feel the blister that developed from not wearing any socks with my gym shoes. My hopes were crushed when I realized that not only was I back in the cemetery, but also, that I was alone there. With my head down, I gathered myself together and went home.

That night I lay in my bed and cried harder than I ever have. I had a hole in my gut where Jonathan used to be, and I didn't know how to mend it. What if I never find Jonathan in heaven? I needed to talk to someone. Oh how I wished I had Alina here. She was such a strong guide for Kenny's spirit, and I needed some guidance. I know I can't tell my grandmother, or ask her for advice. She would definitely let me have it for abusing my powers. There has to be someone who might know what to do, that has more experience than I do. I needed another Pathfinder that could guide me and tell me how this whole thing worked. Then it dawned on me. I did know how to find another Pathfinder. Next Monday at 3:00, I would go to the cemetery and find him.

FORGOTTEN

The rest of the week went by quickly. I knew my time in Tennessee was almost done when I saw granddaddy carrying my suitcases down from the attic. This sight used to make me giddy with excitement. However, this summer was different. This summer changed my life forever and brought magic and fulfillment to my once dull existence. The thought of leaving now made me queasy. I tried to come up with reasons to stay, but couldn't think of any. I was so afraid that once I got home to Arizona all the magic would disappear forever. Either that or I would realize that I could only be a Pathfinder in Halls.

Another problem I would have to deal with is my nosey mom. How am I supposed to have the same kind of freedom at home, as I do here? I would never be allowed to walk around the cemetery alone, or take off on my bike for hours of unaccounted time. I would just have to tell my parents that I was older now and needed some independence. Maybe they would sense in me what I felt inside. I feel I had changed from a quirky, dull, young girl, into an important, experienced young woman. I began to get excited for the anticipation of seeing their reaction to the new me.

Before I knew it, it was Monday afternoon. I told my grandmother I was going to go say goodbye to Gabe and some of the people in the neighborhood. I decided it would be nice of me to stop by and see Gabe. He was sad that I was leaving in a couple of days. I felt sorry for him anyway. While I seemed to grow and mature this summer, he just stayed the same. At least he had peace in his house. I will be forever grateful for that.

It was an awkward goodbye to say the least. Gabe wanted me to stay and hang out, maybe eat dinner at his house, but I had other things on my mind.

"You're always running off somewhere mysterious. I wish you'd let me in on your big secret someday." I nodded to him and gave him a hug, then turned around and walked away. I knew someday he would know my secret, whether it was through fate or trickery, yes, someday he would know.

After a forced hug from my aunt and a high five from my uncle, I started toward the cemetery. Since I gave Gabe his bike back, this was going to be a long brutal walk. By the time I arrived, it was passed 3:00. I was really hoping I didn't miss my chance to tell the other Pathfinder what I thought of him. He was pretty easy to spot, for me anyway. I saw his glow immediately. He was sitting on a bench that was part of a fancy memorial plot. I don't think he saw me; he was staring intently at a particular gravestone. I decided to hang back and watch for a minute, hoping that he didn't see my glow until I got a chance to spy on him for a bit.

There was something about him that made me feel at ease. He had an air of experience about him, like an older, wiser brother that knew things that he didn't share with just anybody. Even though I wanted to sock him in the gut, I felt like this might be someone I could be friends with. I sure could use someone to talk to about everything. I crept up behind him, staying hidden, or so I thought. As I leaned in to see what the headstone said that he was looking at, I heard him say, "Do you really think you can sneak up on me with a glow as bright as yours?"

"Oh, I guess not." He caught me off guard so rather than jump him and sock him in the eye, I decided to sit down next to him on the bench.

"I'm mad at you ya know." I stated with gumption.

"I gathered that, but I have no idea why." As he said this, I looked at him for the first time. We were face to face and I was caught off guard by his peaceful aura. He reminded me of a young James Dean. His lip curled up in the corner when he smirked and his hair fell in a dark purposefully messy wave. I was half expecting to see a box of cigarettes rolled up in his sleeve.

"Well, you took Jonathan away from me," just saying the words made me feel foolish. He wasn't mine.

"I have no idea what you are talking about. You mean that kid, from the other day? All I know is that unsettled spirits come to the graveyard all the time, once they have realized that they are dead. This time the one you were talking to was upset and yelling at you. I thought you might have been afraid and I wanted to help. Was he a relative or something?"

"No, and I really don't need to explain anything to you. I just need some answers. First of all, if someone has crossed over and you want to find them, how do you do it?"

"Well, first of all, Miss Pushy, my name is Caleb. What's yours?"

I couldn't believe my ears, I was supposed to be mad at him and telling him what I thought of him and he was calling me names? This was torture. Why can't people just mind their own business and answer simple questions? He reminded me so much of . . . well of myself I guess.

"My name is Samantha, and I'll be the one asking the questions around here." I stood up and got right in front of him, confirming my authority. "You need to tell me how I can find Jonathan in heaven. Tell me everything you know."

I was ready to take mental notes on everything he said. I was determined to get some answers. To my surprise, he just started cracking up. He was laughing right at my face. Now I was really going to punch him!

"You really are a baby Pathfinder aren't you?"

"What are you talking about? First of all I'm not a baby and another put-down is going to earn you a fat lip." I was surprised by my own gumption.

"Okay, Okay, just calm down Samantha. There is no need to get violent. I'm just shocked to hear that you actually fell in love with a ghost."

"That's ridiculous! I'm not in love with Jonathan. I just want to see him to say goodbye and make sure he's okay."

"You know he's fine. You've been there before. Everything he needs is in heaven with him. He obviously doesn't need YOU to be happy." Caleb seemed almost defensive with these words. I wondered why he was being so rude. I just wanted to know how I could see Jonathan again. I was never in love with him. Sure, I loved to spend time with him, but I wasn't doodling his name in my notebook or anything.

I decided that I was approaching Caleb all wrong. He seemed to be one of those macho guys that acts tough. I'll bet I could find a soft spot. That would be my new strategy. "So, whose gravestone are you staring at?" I asked sincerely.

"Oh, I'm just sitting here waiting for my next cross-over. I don't even know this person." I walked closer to the stone and read it aloud. : "Beloved daughter, Julie Hyde 1818-1836. Hmm, that's interesting. Is this a friend of yours?" With that, he got up and walked away, fists clenched. I had a feeling his previous hostility came from a place of familiarity. "I bet you know exactly how I'm feeling, except that

I never got to say goodbye to Jonathan. He just disappeared before my eyes."

"Well if you ask me, you're better off. Just forget about him and move on with your life. Besides, you're never going to see him unless you cross someone over that's in his family. So get over it." Caleb's words struck me like a knife. He was right. I would probably never see him again. I'm sure his family was all gone already. The thought was devastating. I turned around and started walking home, my head down and the tears streaming.

"I'm sorry Samantha, really sorry. I hope you can forgive me. If you ever do, you know where to find me." Caleb's words sent a slight comfort through my body. At least I know another Pathfinder now, someone who might answer questions for me. I believed he was sorry, and knew we would meet again someday.

Rain started drizzling as I exited the cemetery. The whole walk home I thought about Jonathan. He probably wasn't thinking about me though. More than likely, he already forgot about me. I imagined his heaven looked like one of those front porch hoedowns, everyone smiling and celebrating with homemade instruments and bare feet. His sisters were probably the same age as when he left, and his mom was as healthy as a horse. Jonathan's heart is likely filled with joy and satisfaction for the first time in over a century. I needed to let go for now and allow him to exist in peace, I only wondered how I could do this on my own back at home. My heart was in pieces.

GOING HOME

The days passed by quickly. My grandmother started hovering around me and asking me if I was all right. I wasn't used to her attentiveness. I tried to assure her that I was fine, but I wasn't. I did make her reassure me that when I got to Arizona that I would still be a Pathfinder.

Her response was, "There are many roles you may choose in life. You may choose to be a wife, a mother, a friend, a mentor. However, the one thing that you will always be, no matter what your choices are, is a Pathfinder. This will never change. However, the day will come, many years from now, when you will realize that you can't cross people over, because of either emotional or physical pain. This is when you will pass your gift to a loved one in your family. Choose wisely, as this will be the most precious gift you can ever give to someone. I believe I chose wisely, don't you?" She winked and gave me a squeeze then walked away. I never even thought to ask about how I got this gift. My grandmother gave it to me. She was the one I owed my new more meaningful life to. I wanted to share all of these thoughts with her, but since my words never seemed to come out right, I decided I would write her a letter on the plane and mail it as soon as I got home. She would be tickled to get a letter in the mail from me.

On the way to the airport we drove right passed the cemetery. I asked my grandfather to pull over and let me say goodbye to someone. He was about to ask me twenty questions when my grandmother touched his arm and winked at him, as to say, "Just let her go."

I ran as fast I could over to Jonathan's family plot so I could say goodbye; at least see his name one last time. It took several minutes to find his headstone because it was off to the side, not even close to his family's plot. It was old and tattered and read, "Jonathan Terino, Son, Brother, Soldier 1846-1863." I stood there for a moment, tracing his name with my finger. I missed him so much; I wasn't ready to say goodbye to him.

I began walking around his family plot. We never got around to looking at all of the gravestones when he was here with me. There were numerous Terino family members there. The one that stood out to me the most was Zacharias Terino, Jonathan's brother. His family was huge! He himself lived to be 89, and although he was not a doctor, he was a Professor of Science. I wished I could shout to the heavens and tell Jonathan about it! I wondered if he already knew. I scanned the stones and noticed that many of the family members had Jonathan in their names, either as a first or as a middle name. I was delighted to be surrounded by Jonathan's family. I longed to meet all of them, and vowed that someday I would.

When I walked back to the car I finally felt like I could smile again, not a huge beaming smile, but at least a satisfying grin. I knew my experiences in Tennessee were far from over, but I felt like I could go back to Arizona and fill Jonathan's void with a new mission, the mission to help as many people as I could. I would search the heavens for him every chance I got. Who knows, maybe Caleb was wrong. Maybe there was another way to find Jonathan.

By the time we reached the airport it was dark outside. I didn't make my grandparents come inside and see me off; I just gave them hugs and told them I would see them next summer. When I turned to leave, I had this unrelenting feeling that I needed one more hug from my grandmother. I dropped my bag and ran toward her with open arms. I soaked in her glow and her smell and her warmth. I whispered to her shoulder, "Thank you grandmother, I love you."

THE OTHER JONATHAN

It was time to board the plane, something I got used to after all these years of summer traveling. This time things were different though. I held my head just a little bit higher and looked around instead of at the ground as I used to. Since my grandmother passed me her ability to cross people over into heaven as a Pathfinder, my life has new meaning; I took great pride in my closely held secret.

I found my seat, the window as usual, and hunkered down for a nap. I was half-asleep when I felt the plane take off, but it wasn't until the captain turned the cabin lights off that I saw it; Even with my eyes closed, the blinking red light was obvious. It wasn't bright; it was just constant. I opened my eyes, rubbed them a bit, and then peered over the seat in front of mine. About four rows up There was a young man who had a blinking red glow around him. I was obviously the only one who noticed this. What was it? Was this a beacon, calling to me like a guiding light? Was this an alarm, warning me to stay away? The uncertainty was killing me. I had to check it out. I excused myself and crawled over the elderly couple in the seats next to me. Then I walked toward the bathrooms in the front of the plane.

He was sitting next to the window, so I thought maybe it was the light from the wing, but as I got close, I could see it was encompassing this young man. I didn't want to gawk so I kept walking, catching a quick sideways glimpse and continued on to the restrooms. I went inside, pretended to use it and came out, my eyes glued to this red, glowing stranger. As I got closer to him, I thought I was dreaming; I actually stopped and rubbed my eyes again, just in case. It couldn't be. It was impossible! It was . . . Jonathan.

I didn't know what to do. I was about to call his name when he looked up at me and smiled. This wasn't a "hey I missed you, so nice to see you again" smile. This was a "hi there, why are you staring at me" smile. He didn't say a word; he just put his head back down, staring at the notebook on his tray table. I decided to go back to my seat and try to figure out what to do next.

I think I started talking to myself aloud, because the woman next to me said, "What's that dear?" more than once. This boy, just two rows up looked exactly like Jonathan, my lost Jonathan! How could this be? Why was he glowing red? I needed my grandmother, or Caleb, or somebody to help me figure this out. I sat there contemplating for what seemed like hours. I never even got around to writing Grandmother that letter of appreciation. Finally, an opportunity presented itself. He got up and headed to the back of the plane to use the restroom. I decided I would climb back over the elderly couple and stand behind this glowing fellow in the bathroom line.

I walked hurriedly to catch up to him, and then stood close enough to make him uncomfortable so that he had to turn around and look at me. As soon as he did, I ceased the opportunity. "Hi, I'm sorry but you look so familiar. What's your name?"

Nothing could have prepared me for his answer. "Jonathan." The word knocked me off my feet. He bent over to help me up and our eyes locked. I was searching for a shred of recognition, but I got none.

"Are you okay?" he said, almost laughing. "It's an old family name. I didn't think it was scary though." Now I was laughing. We stood awkwardly together until I gathered my thoughts.

"Oh. You look just like someone I know, or knew."

"Really, that's interesting. What's your friend's name, the one I look like?"

"Jonathan, actually, funny isn't it?" I said.

"Weird. That is quite a coincidence. What's his last name?"

I was almost afraid to say it seeing as he looked so much like him. I didn't want to sound like a stalker or something. "Terino," I replied sheepishly.

"Is this a joke?" he started looking around like a hidden camera show snuck onto the plane or something. "My mother's maiden name is Terino. My last name is Shelly. Hey, where did you say your friend was from?"

Suddenly I panicked and just wanted to rewind time and say "Smith" or something. How was I supposed to explain this? "Oh, he's from Tennessee, so it's probably just some weird coincidence. I'm sorry I bothered you." I turned to walk away and he shouted, "Wait! That's where my family is from. This is crazy. I just got back from visiting my grandmother there. I was doing research about my family tree. My parent's sent me out here since I'm interested in becoming a historian. There's a lot of history in the hills of Tennessee. Hey, maybe you know some of my family. Do you want to sit with me and we can swap stories."

Wow. I really got myself in deep this time. I needed to talk to grandmother and figure this out before I go blabbing to a blinking, red stranger. Maybe I was supposed to stay away.

"Well, that sounds great but I am just exhausted." I was hoping he would give up. That didn't happen.

"Do you live near Phoenix? Because I could give you my phone number and you can call me tomorrow. I would really like to talk to you and see if you know any of my relatives."

I agreed to call him tomorrow and he wrote his number on a cocktail napkin with the host's pen. I tucked it away in my pocket and thought about all of the questions I would ask my grandmother.

The rest of the trip I slept, or pretended to sleep. When I got off the plane, I saw my parents waiting with open arms. My dad, with his usual once a year hug, was waiting for me. He always reminded me of a long lost uncle to Elvis, with his black hair swooping down his forehead in a perfect curl. Then my mom, as beautiful as ever, tears in her eyes gave me one of those hugs that inadvertently brought me to tears. She always reminded me of the woman in the beginning of all the movies, the one that looked like a goddess version of the Statue of Liberty. My best friend Casey even came to greet me. It was nice of her to come. Especially since she showered me with compliments about how great I looked and how much more mature I seemed. Casey was one of those friends who felt more like a sister, and hung out with my family even when I was gone. I think everyone should have a friend like that.

It was nice to see them, although I already felt how different life would be now. As we started walking together to get my luggage, I saw Jonathan, the other Jonathan, standing across the conveyer belt, smiling at me. It was hard to see past the red, but I managed to smile and allow myself to feel the connection that immediately bonded us together. His phone number was pulsing in my pocket, as if it had a heartbeat. Not knowing what to do was killing me. I wanted to run over and grab him; just give him that type of hug that would bring all of his forgotten feelings about me back to his soul. I had to work so hard not to touch Jonathan, and now here he stands, practically reincarnated in the flesh, just feet away.

That night, when I finally got home I wanted to call my grandmother and ask her about this red light. I knew she would have answers, but I realized it was too late to call her. I settled in for bed and thought about all the questions I had. As I drifted off to sleep, I thought about the Jonathans, both of them. No matter what Grandmother said, I would keep them in my life somehow, even if it were from a distance.

SEARCHING THE HEAVENS

I woke up by the sound of the phone. I heard my mother yell frantically for my father, so I stumbled out of bed to see what was going on. My parents were crying and gasping, mumbling to each other, in a voice too low for me to understand. Then dad picked up the other phone, and they were whispering and asking questions like, "How did it happen? How can we help? What can we do?"

As soon as they hung up, I knew. It was my grandmother, my spirit guide, and she was gone. The news hit me like a thousand bee stings. I wanted to throw up. I needed her! She can't leave me! What was I supposed to do? Then I remembered. She would be in my heaven and I can go there anytime I crossed someone over. For now, I cried myself to sleep, missing my grandmother already.

The aftermath of my grandmother's sudden death was heart breaking. My parents were a wreck. My father, who was her second oldest son, tried to be strong for his sisters. He was always trying to hide his emotions, making everything into a joke. His ability to make people laugh came in handy most of the time. This time, he was at a loss for words. He was a tall sturdy man that had a strong work ethic and a love of crossword puzzles. He was always having fun and finding ways to entertain people, but I can't remember ever seeing him cry before.

It occurred to me that this was our first real experience with death as a family. Last year at this time I would have had my head buried in a pillow, crying my eyes out, scared to death. I never really understood death before I became a Pathfinder. I was scared of what eternity meant and where people went when they died. Now, I know my grandmother is fine in her own personal heaven. She is with everyone she loves and everything that makes her happy. Although I was sad, this thought comforted me a bit.

I tried to be strong for my mother, who always had a close relationship with my grandmother. She was the rock in our family, but this sudden death took the wind from her sails. My mother was one of those women who always seemed to have it together. She was a girl scout in her youth, so she was always prepared. She went into automatic preparation mode, making phone calls, digging out old papers, and taking charge of the situation. Halfway through the day she collapsed with exhaustion. This time she needed help and I was the strongest one in the house. I tried to help her see heaven through my eyes, without revealing any of my secrets, of course. She must have thought I was in denial or acting foolish, because she sent me off to take our dog, Stinker, out for a walk.

I watched my mom through the kitchen window as she cried, and wanted to comfort her. She was always there to comfort me and this time I had the key to helping her understand. She was a lot like me in the sense that she didn't understand death and wasn't sure about the whole heaven and hell matter. I think that's why she only went to church on certain days. I was amazed to realize that I was not the only one confused about death and the after-life. Then I wondered why other Pathfinders didn't help put people's minds at ease by revealing information. Maybe they had and were consequentially locked up in a loony bin somewhere in the hills of Minnesota. I decided to follow the rules, too.

My parents finally sat me down at dinnertime and explained what happened to my grandmother. On their way home from the airport my grandmother fell asleep in the car. My grandfather didn't want to disturb her so he let her sleep until they got home. When he tried to get her to wake up, she wouldn't budge. He drove her to the hospital and she was pronounced dead on arrival. She just went to sleep and never woke up. It sounded so peaceful, yet so lonely. My head swirled with feelings of sadness, sympathy, and complete heartbreak. Even though I knew she was in a beautiful place, I couldn't help but miss her. I felt so selfish for wanting her to remain here, in Halls, where I could visit her every summer. I longed to swing on the porch with her and crack green beans. I wished I had known that this was to be the last summer I would spend with her here. She must have known.

I was so grateful that Grandmother helped me understand death and passed me her gift before she died. I couldn't wait to see her and ask her questions I deeply needed to know. Did she choose to die at that moment? Is that something Pathfinders have the power to do? Did it hurt? Will I be able to see her anytime I want? Will she be in my heaven, too? What about Granddaddy? My heart sank with the thought of him all alone. I wish I could take him with me to visit Grandmother.

I needed to see her and I needed answers, but they would have to wait. That night, we all packed up for a whirlwind 3-day trip to Tennessee to attend my grandmother's funeral. It was filled with tears, food, family reunions, and Pathfinders. I was in awe of how many elderly Pathfinders were there. They mostly just shook my hand with encouragement and told me she would always be with me. One in particular stood out though, as he never approached me. He just stood in the background and kept an eye on me. It was a little creepy, I have to admit.

On our last day in Tennessee, we finally had some down time. I wanted to go to the cemetery to find a wondering soul, but Gabe came by to hang out. I was too tired to do much so we just hung out in the garden and reminisced about Grandmother. He was beside himself with pain over her death. They were very close and he was already so lonely. All I could do was sit with him and comfort him the best I could.

When dusk rolled around, I offered to walk him halfway home. I told myself that if the opportunity arose, then I would find the energy to cross someone over. I really needed to see my grandmother.

On my way back to the house, without Gabe, the creepy old Pathfinder was standing a few houses away from my grandmother's. I quickened my pace, unsure of what he wanted. He must have seen my discomfort and called out, "It's all right. I just wanted to talk to you, Samantha." His familiar glow made me stop and realize that he was a friend and not someone to be scared of.

"Hi. Can I help you with something?" I asked.

"Yes, actually, I hate to ask you this, right after your grandmother's passing and all, but I need your help."

"My help, sure, what can I do?" I asked, getting intrigued.

"I just moved into an old house that's been abandoned for some time and it seems to be pretty well haunted. I'm just too old to help them out. Besides, they're not like the spirits I've encountered in the past."

"How do you mean?"

"Well, they seem to be fully aware of their predicament, but instead of trying to get help moving on, they just play pranks all day and night. I can't even invite company over. I've tried talking to them; I'm assuming there's more than one with all the activity going on. I've already passed my gift onto my son who isn't available to help me. I hate to ask you this, seeing as how you've been through so much, but I figured you'd want to go see your grandmother anyway. This could be your ticket."

"I do want to see my grandmother, but it sounds a little scary." This was the first time I had thought about an unsettled spirit as scary, since the first trip to heaven. I have to admit I was captivated. I missed that feeling of the hair standing up on my neck when I thought about ghosts. As tired as I was I agreed to do it. He gave me his address, just across the railroad tracks, and I told him it would have to be later, when I could sneak out of the house.

We had to pack our bags that night. We would return to Arizona in the morning. I was afraid to fall asleep that night, knowing how tired I was there was no way I would be able to wake back up and go help the man out. So I paced around the room for a while, remembering all the fun times I had with Jonathan in there. I could almost imagine him there jumping on the bed. All the feelings rushed through me again and I was even more anxious to see Grandmother in heaven. I decided to go earlier than planned over to the man's house.

I was braver than ever as I walked along in the middle of the night. It was quiet for a Tennessee summer night. I didn't even hear the crickets or the locusts. As I approached the address of the old man's house the noise level raised in a hurry. I could see through the windows that there was a lot of commotion going on inside. There were sprits racing around like shooting stars. It looked like a war was going on inside. My presence was noticed immediately and I saw one of the spirits bolt though the house shutting all the windows. The man came outside, probably for some peace and saw me standing there in awe.

"Do you see what I mean now?" he said, looking exhausted.

"Wow! I've never seen anything like this. You must have a whole herd of spirits in there. Do you have any idea who they are or what they want?" wishing I could just turn around and walk away.

"No, I just know that there are about five of them. There is a leader, I hear him while I'm sleeping. They want me to leave, they say it's their house and I'm an invader. Their plans are getting more and more hostile. I would move out if I could, but I can't afford any place else, and you know as a Pathfinder I can't consciously leave them to wander here any longer. I've tried talking to them, but they don't listen to me at all. I need someone quick and young to catch them and cross them over, even if it's against their will."

I wondered why he never found Caleb. He seems like he would be better suited for this job, but I needed to get to my grandmother to find out about the other Jonathan; so I took a deep breath and went inside. I took notice of all the broken items scattered about and glanced back at the old man. He shook his head as to confirm that this was the work of the restless spirits. I began walking up the stairs to the attic, confident I would find them there, and like a bolt of lightning, a wad of light shot right passed me.

There was something frigid about these spirits. They didn't give me the same feeling as the other souls I have encountered. One broke free of the pack and stood at the bottom of the steps looking curiously at me. It was a young girl about my age; but her face looked hard and tired. Her glare sent shivers up my spine. Again, I was paralyzed. This girl began floating up the stairs, never releasing her stare. Her eyes were glowing yellow and her teeth looked like she was snarling. Had she gone mad? All of these years of wandering must have hardened her spirit. She stopped one stair away from mine and lifted her hand toward my face. I wasn't sure if she was going to touch me or strangle me. She was so close I could make out freckles on her cheeks. The glow that came from behind her intensified and I could feel the coldness in the air. The others were behind her trying to pull her away from me. Then her tears began to fall and I reached out and touched her hand.

We were all transported instantly, still grasping each other's hands. Then like a carnival ride, each of the spirits went in different directions. I was still holding on to the young freckled girl when we arrived into her heaven. Her heaven looked exactly like the house we had just left, only it was daytime and the decorations were clearly not the same. She was beaming with glee as she ran around touching everything, and calling out for her mother. A woman in a blue-checkered apron came running out of the kitchen and they embraced. They talked about how much they had missed each other. Then her mother led her into the kitchen where the rest of her family sat around a large table set for a Thanksgiving feast. I was invited to stay, but kindly declined. I was on my own mission.

I closed my eyes and thought of my grandmother. I felt the wind through my hair and the movement of my spirit into a new heaven, one that looked like a painting of a place that could soothe anyone's soul. There was a woman there who looked like the picture that hung on my grandmother's wall ever since I could remember. She noticed me instantly and ran to me, a smile beaming across her face. It wasn't until she said my name that I realized it, this was my grandmother. She was at least 40 years younger than when I saw her last. Even her arthritic fingers were now long and nimble. Her hair was full and bounced in the wind, and her skin was like milk, pure and flawless. I was so happy to see her, even if she did look different. She sat me down on the picnic blanket under a tree. I couldn't help staring at her.

"I've been waitin' for ya," she said, as she winked and grasped my hand. "I'm so sorry I left you like that, you just never know when it's your time to go."

"So you didn't know you were going to die, Grandmother?"

"Oh no dear, that's not something we have any control over. I did have a feelin' it was comin', which was why I passed you the gift this summer. I just had to hold on long enough to pass on my gift when I felt you were good and ready."

"Grandmother, I have so many questions, I don't even know where to begin."

"Well dear, some things you're just gonna have to find out for yourself you know. But I will always be here when you need me."

"I need you now grandmother. Can you help me with just one thing? I met someone on the airplane ride home last week. He was surrounded by a blinking red light, and I don't know what that means. Is this person someone I should stay away from, or is he someone I should help?"

"My goodness Samantha, this is very rare. I've actually only heard stories about situations like this. The boy you met, is there somethin' special 'bout him. Is there anything else you're not tellin' me 'bout him?"

"Well, I don't want you to get upset or disappointed, but do you remember the old house across the street from your friend? This boy looks just like the spirit that I met at that house. They even have the same name. I sort of befriended that spirit and we spent a lot of time together. But he got crossed over by another Pathfinder before I had a chance to say goodbye or anything."

Grandmother's look turned serious as she said, "Samantha, you need to be careful 'bout how close you get to these spirits. You know you can get lost. This red light you see, this is a sign that was sent from someone in heaven. Your friend must want you to help this boy or stay with him for some reason. The message is somethin' that you will need to figure out. Let me warn ya though that this spirit could get ya lost forever. Think of your parents and how devastated they would be if they lost ya'."

"Why can't I just find him in heaven and ask him myself?" I wondered aloud.

"Honey, you can only move through the heavens of those you have crossed over or anyone in their family. This boy you told me 'bout, the one from the airplane, he must be connected in some way to the boy who has crossed over; they may even be blood relatives." I wasn't surprised to hear this information. I could tell just by looking at the other Jonathan, that he was a relative of my Jonathan. What I still wasn't sure of was what the message meant. I vowed to figure it out immediately.

Grandmother and I sat quietly together listening to the river that was just beyond the picnic blanket. As I looked around my grandmother's heaven, I noticed there were two sets of plates and glasses, as if she were waiting for someone. I wondered where everyone else was. Where were all of her friends and family members who had passed before her? I asked her to explain where we were and why she was alone.

"I'm waitin' for someone special. He should be here soon. As far as everyone else is concerned, they are on the other side of the hill, enjoyin' themselves." I looked past the tree and saw what appeared to be an old-fashioned county fair. There were some rides and real horses, and tons of people. It was a beautiful sight. To think, all my life I have been scared of death, unsure of what came next. Now I know that when your physical life is over, there is another world that can make you just as happy.

"It's time for you to go back Samantha. Remember, if you stay in heaven too long, you risk forgettin' 'bout the physical world. That is where you belong. Now go back and give your mama and daddy a hug for me. And tell Granddaddy I'll be waitin' patiently." Grandmother hugged me for a long time, transferring her warmth and peacefulness to me so that I can pass it along to my family. I didn't want to leave but I knew I would see her again soon.

"I love you Grandmother!"

"I love you too honey!"

With that, I closed my eyes and transported myself back to the old house across the tracks. I was in an awkward position on the stairs when I woke up. The old Pathfinder was waiting patiently at the bottom of the steps. As I came to, he walked up and held out his hand to help me to my feet. He thanked me sincerely and walked me home.

I must have gotten about 15 minutes of sleep when it was time to go to the airport again. Through the hustle and bustle of the day, I almost forgot about grandmother's message. I sat next to my granddaddy on the porch and took his hand. I looked into his tired eyes and told him that grandmother would always be with him and that someday they would be reunited forever. He hugged me long and hard and whispered that he would be okay. I swallowed the lump in my throat and walked away. That was the hardest thing I have ever done.

I had one more message to pass along. Before we got in the car, I stopped my mom and surprised her with a big warm hug. She instantly relaxed, and thanked me. We stood arm in arm, staring at grandmother's house. It seemed so different with her gone. My dad noticed us standing together and joined in the embrace. Without really thinking about it I said, "Grandmother wants you to know that she is okay." They both looked down at me and my dad squeezed me a little harder. I think they knew it was true.

DECODING THE MESSAGE

The plane ride back to Arizona was long, but it gave me a chance to think about everything. I decided that as soon as I got home I would call the other Jonathan and see what happens. The words that grandmother and Caleb, the Pathfinder from the cemetery, told me about having to cross someone over from the Terino family in order to see my Jonathan again were ringing in my ears.

Suddenly I realized that this must mean the other Jonathan was going to die. Could this be possible? Is this the type of message I would receive from heaven? I just couldn't believe it was true. There must be some other reason. The urgency to find his phone number and call him increased as thoughts swirled around in my mind. I didn't want to think of him as my ticket into the proper heavenly corridor, but that might just be what it was. In this case, should I risk getting to know him or watch him from afar?

Once we were back at home and settled it was dinnertime. My parents ordered some pizza and we all ate ravenously. It had been a long time since I ate anything that wasn't pulled from a garden. The night was still young and everyone settled in to watch some television. I excused myself from the sofa and went to look for the other Jonathan's phone number. I couldn't remember at first where I left it. I started to panic as I realized that the shorts I was wearing when he gave me his number were probably in the laundry.

I rushed to the laundry room and dug through the pile of mildewing clothes that had been sitting there for several days. It didn't take long to find the shorts because the cocktail napkin with the phone number on it was pulsating in my pocket. If I didn't know any better I would think it was alive. I crinkled it up in my hand to lessen the intensity and went to the kitchen to use the phone. While my parents were distracted by the 5:00 news, I picked up the receiver and nervously punched in the number.

"Hello." The voice of a soft-spoken female flowed through the lines.

I paused for a moment, contemplating hanging up the phone. Then I cleared my throat and said, "Um . . . yes . . . hello . . . is Jonathan there?"

"Sure sweetheart, just a moment." I heard the woman call to someone who must have been close by. "Johnny, you have a phone call dear."

"Hello, this is Johnny." My heart immediately floated into my throat at the sound of his voice. I couldn't believe the similarity between him and my Jonathan; it was uncanny. "Hello, is anybody there?"

"Oh, yes, I'm sorry, I'm here." I had almost forgotten to respond.

"Who is this?" the voice asked.

"This is Samantha, from the airplane."

"Oh my gosh, you called! I thought you forgot about me." He must have turned to the woman who answered the phone, because I heard him say, "Mom, this is the girl I told you about, the girl who knows some of our relatives!" He was genuinely excited to hear from me; this put me at ease.

"So, you go by Johnny, not Jonathan?" I asked, relieved that I didn't have to share his name with my Jonathan.

"Yah, well I try to get people to call me Jonathan, but they're so used to calling me Johnny, that it just seemed to stick."

We continued with idle chitchat for a while. I told him about my grandmother passing away and having to return to Halls. He gave me his condolences and told me about the research he has been doing on his family tree this summer. Then we talked about where we lived. I could tell he wanted to get together, and honestly, I wanted to see him, too. He reminded me so much of Jonathan that I pretended it was him when he started talking. I wondered if he was still blinking red, the image in my head made me laugh a little to myself.

We realized that we didn't live too far from each other. He went to the rival high school though, not mine. I was a little disappointed about that, but I would find time to see him before school started.

We made plans to meet at the Civic Center Library, which was on the trolley line that seemed to be close to the middle of our homes. I had to try to figure out what to tell Johnny when I saw him. I knew that I would feel like I was part of Jonathan's life again just being near him. I couldn't wait to see him again. I'm certain he will ask me questions I could answer but wouldn't know how to explain how I knew so much. My head started to pound from the mixed emotions that were occupying my mind.

I excused myself to my room so I could get ready for the meeting. I was happy to see my mom doing some of the laundry as I walked to my room. Since I hadn't been home for a while, I needed to revisit my wardrobe. I seemed to have a different figure these days. I didn't feel frumpy like I used to. Sifting through my closet from some of my "skinny clothes" was more fun than I remembered. Suddenly I found myself putting outfits together, and trying on skirts. It only took me a moment to realize that I was hoping Johnny would like me for more than just the information I might be able to provide. In a way, I felt like maybe the message I was getting from heaven was that this was my Jonathan, reincarnated into my soul mate. I put these thoughts aside and started working on a way to lie about how I knew about his family.

The next day, while my parents were distracted with catching up on work from the three day unexpected trip, I told them I was going to my best friend, Casey's, house. I was starting to wonder how often I was going to have to lie. I decided to swing by her house on the way to the trolley stop.

Luckily, Casey lived just around the corner from my house. She was getting ready to go shopping for her back-to-school wardrobe. I was grateful that she would be out all day and wouldn't be stopping by to see me, ruining my cover. I offered to stop by later to see what she bought. I was excited for her to have new clothes too, that way we would have more to share. I was certain that we were now the same size. With all the excitement at the airport when she picked me up with my parents, I didn't notice that her hair was significantly shorter than when I left this summer. She had the cutest little bob haircut, making my long hair feel scraggily and lifeless. I need to consider getting a mini makeover before school starts up in a couple of weeks.

When I got to the trolley stop the difference in temperatures between Scottsdale and Halls was painfully evident. I was melting, and my eyes were burning. I pulled my sunglasses out of my backpack and the paper that held Johnny's phone number came out and fell to the ground. As I picked it up, I realized it was no longer pulsating. Instead, it was just faintly glowing red. I guess I solved that part of the puzzle. I was hopeful that I was on the right track to figuring out Jonathan's message from heaven.

It only took about 15 minutes to get to the library. I found Jonathan sitting at a table in the teen room, waiting for me and glowing red. I noticed he was no longer blinking red; it was more like a red hue. I must be getting closer to the answers.

As I moved toward him, Johnny looked up and smiled a welcoming grin. I felt shy for a moment, but couldn't take my eyes off him. It was eerie how he resembled my Jonathan. I wasn't sure if I should shake his hand, give him a hug, or just say hello. Luckily, Johnny took it upon himself to reach out to me for a hug. I embraced him and closed my eyes, pretending he was my Jonathan. I could feel his heart pounding in his chest and felt a sense of familiarity in his presence. It was as if we were long lost friends, brought back together after a lifetime of separation. This feeling made me wonder if my meeting Jonathan was a way to connect with Johnny, rather than the other way around.

As we separated, I looked down at the table Johnny had been sitting at, I noticed tons of papers, and notebooks scattered around the table. I could tell he was serious about researching his family history. He began instantly rattling off explanations and names of relatives that were still living, which bored me a bit. Every time he mentioned the name Jonathan, he asked me if that was the Jonathan Terino, I told him that I knew when we spoke on the airplane. I would shake my head and give him a look of contemplation, as if I were trying to figure out if that was the relative of his, that I knew. When he got to the deceased members of his family, I perked up and started listening. He mentioned that his great-great grandfather was Zacharias Terino and I'm afraid he really noticed my body language change then.

"Did Zacharias have any brothers or sisters?" I asked, hoping he just thought I was curious, or politely staying involved in the conversation. Realizing I was interested in his research, Johnny dug through one of the piles to show me an old photograph of a large family. "This is Zacharias Terino and his children, his wife, and 3 of his grandchildren and this is his sister, Laura. That's my grandfather standing next to him. I love this photograph." He was pointing to each of the family members and saying their names. I just focused in on Zacharias and Laura. This was Jonathan's brother and sister. It was so surreal to be looking at these people and instantly feeling so connected to them.

"Did Laura ever get married?" I asked.

"I don't think so. She lived with Zacharias her whole life. I heard she was a little crazy. I guess she kept a diary and my grandma's going to locate it for me. She said she talked about an older brother named Jonathan, but no one seems to know too much about him. That is why I went to Tennessee this summer. I was trying to find evidence of him and who he might be. He is the one missing part of my research." His words sent goose bumps down my spine. No one knew about Jonathan? How could that be? He was a Civil War soldier! Johnny must have read the angst in my face and started piecing things together.

"Hey, you said you knew a Jonathan Terino. You weren't talking about . . . Nah, what am I saying. He probably never even existed or died over a hundred years ago. How would you know him? Never mind, that was silly of me." He shook off the thought and started searching around for more pictures. I had to tell Johnny about his distant relative that seemed to be lost in the shuffle.

At that moment, I decided that telling Jonathan's story was more important than my inability to lie about my identity. I turned to Johnny and said, "Actually it is the Jonathan I know, and yes, he was Laura's brother. He was a Civil War soldier and died when he was 17. He was a kind and helpful son, a caring and nurturing brother, and a great friend." Johnny was stunned with my words, and instantly began recording everything I said in his notebook.

"Wait a minute. How do you know about Jonathan? My grandmother doesn't even know much about him." His question was expected but still caught me off guard a bit. "Well, I too like to do research and just take my word for it; I am telling you the truth. He was a young brave Confederate Soldier that died after a battle near Fort Pillow. His gravestone is in the county cemetery. Didn't you look there?"

I didn't even notice that he had started digging through a pile of photographs as I was speaking. What he pulled out astounded me. He placed an old photo in front of me and asked, "Could this be Jonathan?" I picked it up gently, as it seemed as fragile as the Mona Lisa.

"Yes, this is him. This is my Jonathan, handsome and young and brave." He was dressed in his uniform, musket held proudly across his chest. I was flooded with emotions and tears began welling up in my eyes. Johnny just stared at me and waited. I knew he needed an explanation, but I had none to give him. I just looked over at him and said, "It doesn't matter how I know him, maybe I will explain this to you someday. Just trust me that the information I am giving you is absolutely true and you should put him down on your family tree, because he was a very important part of your family."

Johnny picked up his pencil and wrote some more. I continued telling him the stories that Jonathan told me about life on the farm near the Mississippi River. I took great joy in watching Johnny add Jonathan's name to an empty branch on his family tree. I was also glad to be able to clear Laura's name and assure him that she was not crazy; she was just funny. She was the sister who would pretend to be the family pet, just to get everyone laughing at a time of great sadness. Yes, she did have a brother named Jonathan that took great care of her.

When Johnny was finished transcribing my stories he said, "I have something that you might like to see." With that, he pulled out a picture that was very old and torn on all four corners. "My grandmother found this in her attic. She lives in a house that has been in the family for generations. I believe this is a picture of a part of Jonathan's family." Before he got a chance to point anyone out, I knew immediately and said, "Claire!" I knew it had to be her. She was young, pregnant, and smiling. She was standing with who I would assume was her husband and her father, Jonathan's father. Johnny's puzzled look grew more intense so I looked up at him and gave him a smirk. He had no idea how much all of this meant to me. I felt like I was at a family reunion. Maybe he did know how much it meant, he too was reuniting with part of his family, the part that was almost forgotten.

KEEPING THE SECRET

The time had passed quicker than I could have ever imagined. It dawned on me that my parents thought I was at Casey's house, and would call her if I were running late for dinner. Dinner at my house was a non-negotiable. You were to be at home every night with your hands washed and your appetite ready by the time the street lights turned on to have dinner together at the table. I told Johnny I had to get going. I took one last look at the family photographs as I stacked them up and slipped them into his bag. My heart fluttered a bit and a smile grew on my face, as I pushed back a tear. Someday I will find a way to see Jonathan and his family, even if it takes forever.

My thoughts were interrupted by Johnny who I hadn't noticed was staring at me. "Samantha, why are you so emotional about my family? What is it that makes you feel so connected to them? Your convictions seem as strong as mine, yet you're not related to them and you've never even met any of these people." Johnny sounded both intrigued and apprehensive when he said this to me. Although I had hoped he wouldn't be quite so inquisitive, he continued with his questions, unwilling to simply take my word for it. "I can sense that there's something special about you, Samantha, but I can't put my finger on it. Are you some kind of psychic or medium or something?" If only it were that easy to label or to explain.

"No, Johnny, I'm just someone who likes to learn the history of people who have passed away. Lighten up. Can't you just be happy that I can tell you about your family?" I wondered how long I could keep my secret from him. I could feel our bond growing stronger.

We finished packing all of his research and notebooks away and began walking together through the library. It felt good being with Johnny, especially since he smiles at me every time our eyes meet. I wondered how he felt about me. Was he just intrigued by me or was there something more? He began talking about his parents and his sister as my mind wandered away. I wasn't listening to him at all. His red glow was still faded but was definitely there and definitely distracting. Every time I looked at him, my mind would focus back on my mission to find the message that my Jonathan was trying to send to me from heaven. I wish this whole path finding thing came with instructions.

Just then, a flash of light tore through the front entrance of the library. It made me jump, but didn't faze Johnny. He looked at me funny then kept talking. The light was large, fast, and somewhere outside. I knew what was coming next. Somehow I needed to get Johnny to leave so that I could go find the spirit that just whizzed by. He was already questioning me so I didn't want to freak him out any more than I already had.

"Hey Johnny, you go ahead and go. I need to use the restroom. Can I call you tomorrow?"

"Um, sure, I mean, of course you can. But I can wait for you and walk with you to the trolley stop."

"No thanks. You need to get home, too. I'll be fine. Go ahead and go, really." Although I was happy that Johnny was a gentleman and wanted to walk me to the trolley stop, I was really hoping he would just let me go.

"Okay. Well, call me tomorrow then. Bye Samantha." I watched him walk away his head likely spinning with new information and new questions. As he turned the corner, out of my sight, I took off in the direction the light had gone.

The courtyard outside of the library had tons of trees and statues and buildings. This spirit could be anywhere. As much as I wanted to help, I knew it was getting late and I would have to be headed home. Otherwise these little rendezvous would be halted by my mother. After looking around, felling like I was searching for a lost puppy, I gave up and headed to the trolley stop. While I was walking, I felt like I was being followed. I half expected to see Johnny lurking around watching me. I was afraid to turn around and see who it was. He would really think I was strange if he watched me search around the courtyard like I was. The feeling grew stronger as my pace quickened. There was definitely something following me and the closer it got the warmer my back felt. I stopped abruptly and slowly turned my head. I couldn't believe my eyes. The person following me was a spirit: not just any spirit, but my grandfather.

"Granddaddy, what are you doing here? How did you get here? What happened?"

"Well, darlin', I'm not too sure myself. Your grandmother told me the night we dropped you off, just before she passed away, that if I ever get lost and can't find my way that I need to look for you. I thought she was crazy as the dickens when I heard that. But here I am."

"But how did you get here . . . to Arizona . . . to the library?"

"I thought you'd know the answer to those questions. I do believe I had a heart attack in my chair, 'because I couldn't move and couldn't reach the phone. Then suddenly I was as light as a feather. I saw myself slumped over in my favorite chair and thought I was dreamin'. Your grandmother used to say to me that sometimes people get lost when they die and they just needed to find the right path to follow to get back home. Therefore, I figured this was what she meant and I went to find you. I just started runnin' and wondered how I would find you and suddenly I was here. I feel like a youngster, with a new set of lungs and a brand new ticker!" He danced a little jig like a teenager, full of energy. I couldn't help but smile.

"Oh granddaddy, I'm so glad you did find me. You have someone waiting for you in heaven. She cannot wait to see you. Just close your eyes and give me a hug." With one touch, we were whisked away. I never heard my grandfather laugh so loud. He was enjoying the ride and must have known that we were heading somewhere magical. As soon as we arrived in heaven, I realized we were back at my grandmother's picnic site. She was there waiting with open arms. We all embraced for what seemed like forever. As we separated, I noticed that my grandfather looked just like he did in that old hallway photograph. I made a mental note to grab that picture off the wall on my return trip to Halls, Tennessee so that I could always remember them like this.

My grandmother led my grandfather over to the blanket and began telling him everything she had held from him in their physical life. I sat at the edge of the blanket and listened. I watched as they fell in love all over again, staring into each other's eyes. They both looked like they were in their twenties, with a glow that made them look like dreamy old-fashioned movie stars.

As much as I wanted to stay with them and enjoy their youthful spirits, I knew I had to get back. There was something pulling me back. It was a feeling as if I forgot to turn the stove off or something. It became more urgent with the passing moments. I said goodbye to my grandparents and assured them that I would visit any chance I got. But before I could close my eyes, my grandmother said, "Guard you secret well darling'; there are challenges coming your way."

I didn't understand her cryptic message until I reopened my eyes back in the physical world. Johnny was standing over me, frantically calling my name. He had pulled me up into a sitting position. I realized that I had been lying in the grass near the parking lot. I guess I was lucky that I didn't call any more attention to myself. Knowing how the process works by now, I knew I had only been out cold for a minute or so. Time in the physical world practically stands still when I crossover. I had to think of an explanation quickly, but my body beat me to it as my stomach chose that particular moment, in Johnny's arms, to growl louder than thunder.

"Oh my, I must have fainted. I was hungry and my insulin is probably quite low. I better get something to eat." I may have sounded a little too comfortable with fainting by using that explanation.

"You scared me to death. It looked like you were talking to someone and suddenly you dropped like a ragdoll onto the grass. That was really weird! You were talking about your grandfather while you were unconscious. What were you dreaming about?"

"Were you following me Johnny?" I gave him a flirtatious smile to change the mood of the conversation.

I must have embarrassed him, because his grip on my upper body loosened up at that moment.

"Well, I guess so. I am sorry; it's just that you fascinate me. I can't figure you out. Now I'm really confused. But I think we need to get you something to eat before I have to go scooping you up off the ground again." It was sweet how concerned he was about me. I decided to ruin my appetite and grab a hot dog with him at the stand near Old Town, Scottsdale.

I did not escape his questions for long. He insisted on knowing what I was talking about while I was unconscious. I told him I did not remember, leaving him with unanswered questions. He eventually moved on to telling me some of the history of the old buildings we were passing by. It was amazing how time flew by when I was with Johnny. I was able to forget, even if it was for just a few moments, that my grandfather had just passed away.

When we finished our food, I said a quick "good-bye" and ran to catch the trolley that was about to leave the stop. My stomach began to churn. I wasn't sure if that was from the hot dog or the fact that I was about to face my parents who were going to be heart-broken about my grandfather. I knew it was hard for them to leave him in Halls and were thinking about having him come live with us. They will feel guilty for not insisting on it.

THE RETURN TRIP

As expected, my parents were completely devastated by the news of my grandfather's passing. I had to drum up some tears so I didn't seem strange or insensitive to my parents. Inside, though, I was so happy for my grandparents. They were together, youthful and happy. I longed to tell my parents what I saw. The next morning I decided I would try to tell my parents that I had a dream about my grandparents.

I had always had some crazy dreams. Some of my dreams even came true. One time I had a dream that I was at my dad's office playing basketball on this old hoop that was nailed to the roof of the building in the back alley. Suddenly a car appeared, facing me. It revved up its engine and drove full force toward me. I couldn't run or scream and I woke up as soon as it was about to hit me. The following Thursday, a little girl was hit by a car in that same alley. My parents were really freaked out, but they started paying better attention to my dreams.

Maybe I could comfort them by telling them how happy and youthful they looked in my dream. I sat them both down at the table, trying not to cry as I looked into their sad eyes, and I told them about the "dream." I described my grandmother's heaven exactly as I had seen it when I was with her. Then, I told her about their romantic picnic and how dreamy they looked. My mother reached across the table and touched my hand, thanking me from the depth of her heart. My dad sobbed a bit harder, but squeezed out a smile from the corner of his mouth. It didn't take long to get out of the mourning mode and into the business mode. We had to prepare for yet another trip to Tennessee.

There was only a week before school was going to start, so my parents wanted me to stay home and get ready. However, there was no way I was going to miss the opportunity to go back to Halls. It felt more like home than Arizona. I had to go back. Besides, I needed to get that picture from my grandparent's hallway.

I decided to call Johnny before the hustle and bustle of getting packed up began. He must have been sitting on the phone, because it barely rang once and he answered.

"Samantha?"

"Yes, it's me."

"I've been waiting for your call. I told my parents about your stories and they called my grandmother. She told me that she had a trunk in her attic that belonged to Jonathan's mother. She said I could have it!"

"That's great!" I said, trying not to sound too excited, as to make him even more suspicious. "I have to tell you something though. My grandfather passed away yesterday and we are going back to Tennessee for the funeral. We leave at midnight tonight."

"Oh no, I'm so sorry. Wow, both of your grandparents dying so close together must be really hard on you." Johnny's concern again surprised me. He was so caring and genuine. I began falling for him at that very moment. Most of the boys I knew didn't care about anything but skateboards and MTV. Johnny was different. I reassured him that I was okay and my family was dealing with it well. I told him we believed they united in heaven and are together, in a better place now.

He apologized again and we sat on the phone for a few minutes in an awkward silence. He suddenly broke the silence with a renewed enthusiasm to his voice. "Hey, I have an idea that might take your mind off of the tragedies that your family is facing. Maybe while you are back in Halls you could go to my grandmother's house and meet her. You could go through the trunk and get whatever you think we might want out of there. I'll go ask my mom what she thinks about that idea. Then I can get her address and give it to you. Can I call you right back?" I didn't get a chance to respond, he knew what I was thinking.

He hung up and this time I was sitting on my phone waiting for it to ring.

It did not take long for Johnny to call me back. This time he was really excited. Apparently, his grandmother offered to give him the whole trunk. He gave me the address and told me that I could stop by anytime. He wanted me to call him as soon as I could to tell him what treasures I had found. I promised I would. We talked a bit longer about my grandparents and about school. He wasn't very excited about starting school this year either. We both agreed that usually at this time in the summer we are ready to get back to school to see our friends. However, this year high school seemed trivial. In my case, my whole world had turned upside down in a matter of a couple of months. How was I going to concentrate at school with spirits and Johnny on my mind? We both agreed that we wished we went to the same school.

I had just fallen asleep on the couch when it was time to head for the airport. I ran to my room to grab the address of Johnny's grandmother and was surprised to see that it too had begun to glow red. I couldn't believe my eyes. I almost forgot about the message with Johnny not in my sights. I held tight to the address and became even more anxious to get to Tennessee.

The plane ride was quick, as I slept the whole way. We got there at dawn and rented a car to drive out to Halls. When we drove up to my grandparents' house reality hit me. This would be the last time I would ever come to Tennessee to visit my grandparents. What would happen to their house and their garden? Now the tears began to fall, and they were not forced. I wished I was older and could live here. Maybe my parents would try to keep it in the family. Being in heaven makes you forget about all things physical, but I would love to tell my grandparents that their house was being taken care of and someday maybe I would live there and tend to their garden and their orchard. For now, I just ran into the house and grabbed that old photo from the hallway that mirrored my grandparents' new heavenly appearance.

The wake and funeral were a blur. It was filled with tears and hugs, but no pathfinders. It was very different from my grandmother's funeral. Everyone seemed to be a little bit happier this time. I think it was because they knew he belonged with my grandmother. Many people wanted to believe that when we die we go to a better place. A place they call heaven and imagine is beautiful and serene. I just happen to know it is true and this makes me stronger than the rest.

While my parents were busy talking with the neighbors, figuring out what to do with the house, I went outside to the porch where good old' Gabe sat. I plopped down next to him on the swing: the swing that held so many memories. I gave him a loving punch on the shoulder and he just looked up at me and gave me a fake smile. He loved my grandfather too and was devastated with his passing. I had never seen him so despondent. I reminisced to myself about the times we spent searching his house for ghosts. I giggled to myself about it. I only wish I could ease Gabe's pain and let him know just how happy our grandparents were now that they were together in heaven. In an instant, I could ease his pain. I wished I could take him there and show him Kenny, too. So much death surrounded Gabe and he was really taking it hard.

"Hey Gabe, you should come visit me in Arizona sometime." I hoped the thought of getting out of Halls for a while would make him perk up a little bit.

"Sure. That would be nice. Hey Samantha, do you think you'll ever come back and visit, now that grandmother and granddaddy are gone?"

"Of course I will! Halls is like home to me now. I can't believe I ever fought my parents about coming out here. I wish I could take it all back." We swayed on the swing for a little while, until it was time for him to leave. He gave me an awkward cousin hug and left with his parents. I yelled after him, "I'll call you Gabe!" And I meant it.

Now that things were settling down the butterflies swooped into my stomach. It was time for me to go see Johnny's grandmother and look through the trunk of treasures that awaits me. I told my parents I wanted to go for a walk to the railroad track to flatten some pennies. With the address in my pocket, I walked toward the train tracks, unsure of how I would get to the house. I really wanted to soak up the scenery since there was no telling when I would be back. I studied the old buildings and the beautiful courthouse as I walked by. I was really going to miss Halls. The simplicity of life here was something I had always taken for granted. Kids were always running through sprinklers in their yards, little old ladies were swinging on their porches waving to anyone who passed, and every corner had at least one young boy on a bicycle looking for an adventure.

I kept walking until I reached the track. Some of my grandfather's friends were in the café across from the tracks; I recognized the black suits. I wished I could ask them to point out the direction I needed to go to find the address Johnny gave me.

I started walking toward the Bingo Hall, still unaware of how I would find Johnny's grandmother's house. Suddenly I saw a familiar glow. Caleb was filling up his car with gas on the corner. His glow was faded in the sunlight, but it was there.

I put my hands deep in my pockets and swallowed my pride. The last time we were together in the cemetery we left on good terms, but I was apprehensive to ask for a ride. For some reason Caleb felt like an older brother. Someone I was in some kind of competition with. But the fact was I needed some help. As I got closer to his car, he looked up and started laughing.

"You just can't stay away, can you?" His teeth gleamed in the sun as he smiled.

"What can I say, Caleb, I missed you too much."

"Yeah right, I don't believe that for a second." His banter was fun and lighthearted. I felt like I could ask him for a ride, but knew it would lead to some uncomfortable questions. I asked him anyway.

He agreed to the ride with no hesitation, but when it was time to give him the address, and I pulled out a glowing red piece of paper the questions began.

"What in the world is that?" Caleb said as he snatched the paper from my hand. "Is this a message?"

I realized it was foolish to try to lie to him so I told him everything. . . . well almost everything. His eyes never left the sheet of paper with the address. As I edited my experiences to tell him only what I felt he needed to know, I felt a sense of relief. It was nice to be able to talk to someone that understood, and knew my secret. When I got to the part explaining the address he looked at me and smiled.

"This is amazing. I have heard about messages like this, but never saw one in person. It really is glowing, brightly! Let's get over there and see what this is all about." Caleb said as he started up the engine of his old orange Camaro. It smelled like gasoline and leather, very manly. The rumble of the engine caught the attention of everyone in the area. This car totally suited Caleb. He seemed like he was hungry for attention. If I didn't know him as a Pathfinder, I would probably consider him a meathead. Those are the guys that wear tight shirts and look at their reflection anytime they pass something shiny. He probably wouldn't have paid a bit of attention to me if I were not glowing.

"What do you think the message is? Don't you have any ideas at all, Sam? I can't wait to check this out!"

"Caleb, do you think I could go in by myself? I don't know how to explain your presence, and I'm not sure what I'll find inside. You could pick me up in about an hour or so. Then I'll fill you in on all the details," His eyebrows rose as I told him this.

"Fair enough," he responded. He waited in the car until I got up to the porch and went inside. I turned and gave him a wave to send him on his way.

The house was quaint, obviously old. The outside was a dark green, matching most of the trees that surrounded the street. It resembled the house in the photo that Johnny showed me and I wondered if it was the same house. There was no doorbell, just an old-fashioned knocker that looked like it had centuries of tarnish on it. As the door opened, a short, feeble woman greeted me. She was not like the typical southern women I was related to. She introduced herself and took my hand. Her fingers were ice cold and stiff with arthritis. Her name, I learned, was Vester, an unusual name for an unusual woman. She offered me some sweet tea and pie, of course.

My grandmother used to say, "You should always take an offered cake," which meant it was rude to decline an offering when you are visiting someone's home. So, as much as I wanted to solve this mystery, instead I sat down on her plastic covered couch and ate some apple pie. As we sat there I noticed that the carpets inside were a dark brown shag, the type I remember from my early childhood. She had many crocheted table covers with old photos on top of them.

I also spotted what looked to be a picture of Johnny when he was about 10. She caught me taking a closer look and broke the awkward silence that had been looming over us.

"Johnny tells me you did some research on our family. He sure does love to research. It's amazing you two found each other."

"Yes, it is unusual. But my family has lived here for a long time, just like yours," I said, hoping to change the subject. I was a horrible liar.

"He also tells me your grandparents recently passed. You must be one of the Alleys. I heard Jimmy died and I read that Ellen passed just last week. That must be very difficult for your family. I wanted to get over there and pay my regards, but I've been fighting an awful flu bug." As I listened to her speak I noticed that her eyes were a glossy tone of gray. I wondered if she could see very well. There was another uncomfortable pause in the conversation and I heard some noises coming from upstairs. I assumed someone else was there. Vester noticed the noise, as she too looked up toward the stairway and said, "So you're here to take the trunk I understand."

"Oh, well, I wanted to look through it, for Johnny. I don't need to take the whole thing. I know it belongs to your family."

She turned toward me and said in a pleading voice, "Well, until that trunk is removed I can't go into my attic. So it's best you just take it, seeing as no one else has ever wanted it."

"Why can't you go in your attic? Is it that big? Or is it in your way?" I asked, wondering just how huge this trunk is.

"No, it's just time for it to go. I need some peace and quiet and that trunk gives me headaches. I got used to it for a while, but I'm just too old these days." Her explanation left me with even more questions. How could a trunk full of old stuff give someone a headache? I decided it was time for me to go find out for myself. I asked Vester to point me in the right direction of the attic and offered to go up myself so she didn't have to climb the steps. The uneasy feeling that crept into the pit of my stomach replaced the anxiousness of finding the treasures inside.

HIDING PLACES

As I climbed up the stairs, I realized that every time I've gone into a house with stairs, strange things have happened. I almost wished Caleb were here with me. I had a real uneasy feeling. The higher up I got into the attic the colder the air was. I heard Vester call up to me, "Honey, be careful, you might find more than what you're looking for." What could she have meant? As far as I knew, I was going to rifle through an old trunk of photos and baby clothes, maybe some old papers, and hopefully some letters. It was creeping me out to think about what she said, so I ignored her warning and let my excitement rule my emotions. There was no way fear was going to stop me from getting to this trunk.

At the top of the stairs, I found a string dangling from the ceiling. I pulled on it and a light came on. The attic stretched across the entire house. There were no walls, just stuff everywhere. If I had more time, I would probably stay up there for hours just looking through all of these treasures. I wondered why Vester thought one little old trunk would keep her from coming in here. It seems as though the furniture and boxes that were scattered about would be more of an obstacle.

Then I realized what she meant. The moment I walked into the room, I was overcome with emotions. Something about this attic was affecting me emotionally. Did Vester feel this intensity also? I heard noises and figured it was a rat or something. Remembering the pack rat incident at Gabe's house, I knew I had to be on the lookout for flying rodents.

I wasn't sure where to look so I decided to close my eyes and let my emotions guide me. The feeling that I was being pulled in two different directions suddenly came over me. I looked toward my left and didn't see anything that resembled a trunk, but I was drawn in that direction. Then I looked to my right and I saw a trunk. It was not what I expected, but it was a trunk. I pictured some bulky pirate treasure trunk with metal clasps and a big rusted lock. What was more surprising was the fact that it was not blinking red. I thought for sure it would match the address and the phone number, blinking or at least shining a bit.

The pull was undeniable. I followed it to this medium sized, ordinary looking cedar box with the initials "F.T." carved into the side. I remembered the gravestone in the cemetery that read, "Felicia Terino" and knew I had found my treasure. This was it. This was Jonathan's mother's trunk.

I was about to open the trunk when I heard a whimper coming from the corner of the attic. I almost fell to the floor; I was so startled. I called out, "Hello, is someone there?" All I heard were footsteps and more whimpers. I was definitely not alone up there. The question was could there be a spirit up here with me. Could that be what Vester was talking about? I decided I would continue looking through the trunk and see what happened. I wasn't comfortable lurking around in the shadows with all the junk up here. As I opened the lid, the smell of cedar filled my nose. The light was not bright enough to see exactly what was inside, but it was full.

The footsteps started to get closer. I held my breath. The whimpering had stopped, but I heard sniffling. It sounded like a child.

"Mama?" I heard a small voice coming from somewhere behind me. I turned around and whoever it was hid behind a large piece of covered furniture. If it weren't a child's voice, I probably would've ignored it. I wanted to see what was in the trunk. I didn't want to deal with an unsettled spirit right now. Something in my gut was telling me I couldn't ignore this one.

"I'm not your mommy but my name is Samantha. Are you lost?" I said to the furniture. The footsteps took off the other direction. I went to close the lid of the trunk when I spotted a red glow buried deep amongst the belongings in the trunk. I would have ignored it but it seemed to become brighter and brighter as I stood there. It was almost like a laser beam shooting through the debris. I dug through papers and pictures until I reached the source of the glow. It was a letter addressed to Claire and signed by Felicia. It was faded and torn so I had trouble reading it. The letter was dated in May of 1863 and it read:

My Dearest Claire,

You are so young and so precious. I will miss you very much. You are my baby girl and I love you with all my heart. When you get older, I hope that you will know that I loved you and didn't want to leave you. My illness has no cure so I fear I will leave soon. My dream for you is that you live a long happy life full of love. Please take care of your brother, your sister and your father. Someday we will reunite in heaven.

With warmest regards,
Mama

A tear formed as I got lost in the words. This was Jonathan's mother's letter to Claire before she died. Why is it glowing? It became so bright it was like a flare. I held it up toward the ceiling of the attic and looked around the room. I searched and searched, squinting from the brightness of the letter. Suddenly a box moved and I turned and looked that way. I could barely make out the shape of a little hand that was engulfed in a dull light. It was clasping a box in the corner of the attic. I could tell it was the hand of a young child. The fingers were delicate and small. I was torn between helping this young lost spirit and figuring out this bright red message from heaven. My thoughts turned to my grandmother, who would be furious if she knew my contemplation.

"Can I help you find your mother?" I said, using the bright light from the letter to guide my way toward the back of the attic.

"I can't find her," The little voice answered. The tiny fingers slid off the box and I was afraid the child had run away again.

"If you let me, I can help you find your mama. I promise I won't hurt you."

"Is she in that box?" the little voice muttered.

"Which box sweetie, the one I was looking in?"

"Yes. I think she's in that box. I thought she was in heaven. Is heaven in that box?" My heart sank when I heard this scared little voice. I could tell it was a little boy's voice, although I didn't know why he thought his mom, or heaven was in this box.

"Why don't you come over by me and talk for a while?" I wanted to see his face and make him feel comfortable so I could cross him over. "What's your name?"

There was a long silence and I thought I lost him. Suddenly I heard his voice from the other side of the attic, near the trunk.

"Daniel," he said. My heart sank immediately. My head swirled around and I thought I would collapse. The gravestone flashed into my mind.

"Is your name Daniel Jasner? Daniel Jonathan Jasner?"

"Yes, I think so."

I couldn't believe my ears. I was standing just feet away was Claire's son. I just knew it was him. This was Jonathan's nephew! This was the message from heaven. Daniel has been stuck here for over a hundred years and I was sent to find him and bring him home. I dropped the letter and walked slowly toward the scared little boy. His eyes widened as I got closer and he disappeared again.

"I'm so sorry Daniel; I didn't mean to scare you. I know your mother and she has been looking for you. Come with me and I will take you to see her. He appeared before me like a mirage and I reached out to touch him. He hesitantly grabbed my hand and we were off. He was holding me tightly, unsure of what was happening. In a flash, we were there, in the Terino family heaven.

DECISIONS

I don't think my smile could've been any bigger. Daniel and I were greeted like royalty. There were people hugging and kissing us to the point of smothering. This reunion was a long time coming and everyone was waiting to see him. Claire, looking just as I had imagined scooped up her son and twirled him about as he laughed and shouted with joy. Jonathan's parents hugged me and thanked me for bringing home their grandson. It was very exciting to share in this family's joy but someone was missing.

"Where is Jonathan?" I asked.

"He's right here." The voice came from behind me. I turned around quickly and ran towards him ready to wrap my arms around him with no worries. His warmth and happiness radiated from his body. I felt like I was home right there in that moment. I could close my eyes and never open them again, as long as I stayed right here forever. He picked me up off my feet and twirled me, my feet dangling. He set me down and I loosened my grip from around his neck.

"I got your message." I told him, trying not to giggle. We began walking hand in hand away from the house and the family reunion with Daniel. The Terino family heaven was amazing. It was Tennessee in the 1800's on one side and across the meadow was Tennessee in the 1900's. Two worlds together uniting a family that spanned for over a century. They were just as connected in death as they were in life. Everyone was happy and celebrating.

He led me to a shady spot under a huge weeping willow tree. We sat together as close as two people could get without becoming one. We watched the celebration from afar, as I filled him in on my adventures in the physical world. He was so at ease now, unlike when we were together away from heaven. We laughed until we cried when we reminisced about our time together there. We talked about all of my Pathfinder experiences and how it had changed my life. Then I told him about Johnny and he perked up.

"Is he your boyfriend now?" He asked, trying to make me blush and wrapping his arms tightly around my waist.

"No Jonathan. He is very nice; he looks just like you! It's weird." Our faces were so close I thought he was going to kiss me. It was amazing how alive he felt in my arms, not to mention how alive I felt. The euphoric feeling I get when I am in heaven is intoxicating.

"Well, you might want to give the guy a chance. Maybe our meeting was not only for Daniel, but also to bring you two together." He sounded so much wiser than he did as a wandering spirit. What I was really hoping to hear was, "stay here with me forever and we can be happy together." Instead I heard, "You'll have to go back sometime Samantha and he might be waiting for you."

"What if I don't want to go back? Can't I choose whether I go back or stay here?" I knew the answer to that question but wanted to hear what Jonathan had to say.

"Samantha, your parents just went through two major loses when your grandparents died. They cannot handle losing you, too. As much as I want you to stay, you have an important role in the world and many people need you."

Why does he have to make so much sense these days? Doesn't time stand still while I'm here? Can't I live two lifetimes? I could stay here and be with Jonathan, then go back and it will be as if no time has passed at all. It makes sense to me.

"The longer you stay here, the more likely you are to forget about the physical world, and you will be lost forever." The words were in my head, although the source was unknown. It must have been Alina, my spirit guide, or my grandmother, reminding me not to be selfish.

"I will always be here Samantha. You can come anytime you want now." Jonathan looked pleased with his new knowledge of my abilities.

"Fine, but I want to stay for just a little while longer. I believe that party over there is also for me." I said with my nose in the air. "Let's go celebrate and enjoy the time we have, and then I will make a decision."

He was still apprehensive, but agreed anyway. We raced across the meadow, hand-in-hand, and rejoined the family. I was so excited to officially meet Claire. I had such a special bond with her, although I never even knew her. I was pleased to see that she was in her adult form, rather than the baby that Jonathan remembered.

We all played games, ate food, and talked about the physical world. Jonathan made me retell the story of how we met and we laughed about him looking for his musket. It was a wonderful time. I was trying to forget, or get Jonathan to forget that I needed to go back. As we began walking again, this time across the meadow, I felt a pull. I know it wasn't me trying to go to another location, so it must have been something else. My body, which normally feels nothing but euphoria in heaven, felt violent jerking. I looked at Jonathan, panic-stricken. He was calm and kissed my hand, saying, "I love you Samantha, I will see you again soon. Don't worry, I will be here."

With that, I closed my eyes and stopped fighting the pull. When I woke up, I was in Caleb's car as he drove frantically shouting my name. I was once again furious with him. I punched him as hard as I could in the arm. "Why did you do that? Why did you make me come back? You always ruin everything!"

"Samantha, I waited outside for you for over an hour. I knew something was wrong. When I went inside the old woman was panicking. She thought you were dead. She thought that whatever was in that attic had killed you. When she came outside yelling for help, I calmed her down and said I would take you to the hospital. What else could I have done?"

"Oh Caleb, it was wonderful there. Jonathan was better than I remembered. He said he loved me." As soon as the words escaped my lips, I regretted saying it. Caleb slammed on the breaks and turned to me, face to face.

"Look Samantha. You cannot let the euphoria you feel when you are in someone's heaven make you forget about the physical world. That's not how it works."

"I know Caleb but I just can't help it. I feel complete when I am with him. We were meant to be together. I know he says he wants me to move on, but I feel it from him too, he wants me to stay with him."

"You are too important to this world. You have a gift that will settle spirits that have been wandering for even longer than the family you helped today. Didn't it feel great to help them? You cannot throw it away. Please Samantha, think with your head, not with your heart. Trust me on this!"

He was right and I knew it. Just then, I got an idea. What if I didn't throw it away? What if I passed it on to someone that I thought would be able to handle it as I have. I pushed this thought into the back of my mind for now and kept it to myself. I did feel awfully selfish and knew I was being ridiculous, but I just couldn't help it.

We both sat silently and I could hear him breathing heavily. He was upset about this. What's it to him anyway? It's my life and I can do what I want. I wanted to know why he cared so much, but the cedar smell coming from the back seat of Caleb's car distracted me.

"The trunk . . . You got it?" I shouted.

"The old lady wouldn't let me leave without it. She was convinced that it was haunted. Little did she know; she was right!" Caleb laughed to himself.

My thoughts turned to Johnny and again my heart was filled with joy. I couldn't wait to show him everything I found and see the satisfaction in his eyes. I wished I could tell him everything that happened to me today. Again, I had to edit. Only Jonathan knew my secrets. Surprisingly, I was anxious to call Johnny. He has probably been sitting on the phone for the past two days, just waiting for my call. I have to admit that I missed Johnny and was excited to see him.

HOME

I decided to introduce Caleb to my parents so that he could help me with the trunk and get a glimpse of my life. I knew how nosey he was, so I supposed it was inevitable anyway. I told my parents that I bought it at a yard sale down the street and Caleb was nice enough to haul it home for me. They were grateful but curious. They had no idea where I would get the money for this, nor why I would want it. My dad, the history buff wanted to search through it, but I convinced him to wait until we got home.

    I sent Caleb on his way and gave him a hug. I know he cares about me and wants me to be smart about my decisions and that made me feel like I wasn't alone without my grandmother's guidance. I wanted to feel certain that I would see him again so I told him to come to Arizona someday and I would show him around town. I wrote my phone number on his hand with a pen and told him to keep in touch. He agreed and gave me a wave and said, "See you sis." That was the cutest thing he has said since we met, and it was true. He was like a big brother, always looking out for me. I was glad to know Caleb.

We spent the next day packing up the house and closing it up until my Aunt, who lived in Georgia, could come out and take over. Luckily, the family wanted to keep the house in the family and decided to keep it as a vacation home. I didn't feel as connected to the old place anymore, though. Everything I needed, including my grandparents' photo was in a cedar trunk, my suitcase, and my heart. The thought of being able to come back to Tennessee where my journey began was comforting though.

I was getting used to this plane ride, so the trip home was quick and easy. I had already called Johnny from Tennessee so he knew I would be home today. He also knew I didn't die, as his grandmother thought. The phone was ringing when we got inside the house. I picked up the receiver and sure enough, it was Johnny. He wanted to see me and check out the trunk so he arranged to come pick it up and hang out for a while. I told him to come on over and gave him directions. It just about killed me to think that I couldn't tell him the story of how I got the trunk and the real reason I was meant to find it. This was so much more compelling than any of the articles it held.

My parents were exhausted so I didn't get into the whole story about the trunk and my mysterious new friend, Johnny. Instead, I just told them I was giving it to a friend of mine that will take it to the museum and put it on display. They were impressed with that. I heard my dad tinkering around in the garage earlier this morning, so I figured he had finally satisfied his curiosities about the trunk. My parents went to the door when Johnny rang the bell and introduced themselves to him. My dad told us that there were some great treasures in the trunk and he was very impressed with our decision to donate it to the museum. Johnny gave me a funny look and I shooed my parents back into the house.

Johnny couldn't decide if he was happier to see the trunk or me. Luckily, he chose to give me a hug before asking about the trunk. We both excitedly took off for the garage to check it out. As soon as I saw it, I felt a rush of emotions. I remembered everything that had happened when I first saw it in the attic of his grandmother's house. My heart was beating so loud that I could hear it in my ears. It no longer had a red light shining from within, which saddened me a bit. I was hoping there would be some other sign from heaven that Jonathan was with me.

We rifled through the treasures, each one more interesting than the first. We found tin type photos, clothing, letters, journals, tools, and a beautiful handmade quilt. The letters and journals were all I cared about and the pictures interested Johnny the most. We got some folding chairs out of the laundry room and hunkered down for what would end up being four hours of nostalgic bliss. Johnny brought his backpack so he arranged the photos in an album he had created to depict the lineage of the Terino family tree. Then he carefully scribed the names of the family members in their rightful place on the family tree sketch. He was completely satisfied with the treasures I retrieved for him.

I read and reread some of Felicia's journals, focusing mostly on anything having to do with Jonathan. She must have written every Sunday since she was about fourteen. I loved reading about her childhood and meeting her husband and the birth of all of her children. It was as if I was there experiencing it with her. I decided that next time I went to visit Jonathan in heaven I would sit down with Felicia and reminisce with her.

By the time we were finished, the muscles in my face were aching from smiling and laughing with Johnny. He was so easy to be around, I felt like he was a male version of myself. I truly enjoyed his company and was saddened when it was time for him to leave. We were going to have to start school the next day so we both knew it would be a while until we saw each other again. When we heard his mom honk from outside of the garage, he pulled me in for a hug. This wasn't a quick 'see you later' hug. This was a long, solid, connecting hug. I almost felt like I was floating for a minute. This time I didn't picture Jonathan in my mind; Johnny filled my thoughts instead. With his slow release, ours eyes met and I'm sure I blushed. He kissed my cheek and left.

I thought about Johnny and the kiss all night as I prepared for school. I desperately wanted another one. As excited as I felt about it, I also felt a bit guilty. How much does Jonathan know, sitting up there amongst the clouds? I wonder if he is thinking about me at all. The longer I was away the more he would forget about me, I was certain of that. I wasn't going to let that happen. As soon as I could, I would go to him. I needed to see if he missed me. Maybe he changed his mind and wanted me to stay there with him, now that we were separated for a while.

On the other hand, Johnny was here, in the flesh. This wouldn't be a forbidden relationship. Being in the physical world wasn't as bad as it used to be. I had Johnny now and wouldn't be able to give that up too easily. My life was full of adventure and mystery, a far stretch from my life before this gift. Geez, couldn't I have both? I fell asleep that night and dreamt about Jonathan and me living in heaven together, forever frozen in time as youthful teenagers. I imagined how much fun we would have traveling to different heavens. I could introduce him to my grandparents. We would never age, never get hurt, and never be sad.

When I woke up, I was sad, to the point of tears. It was never going to happen; Jonathan wouldn't let it. He wanted me to live my life here and join him when the time comes. I needed to fulfill my duty as a pathfinder and pass it on to someone when I was too tired to continue. I would have to accept that for now. In the meantime, filling up my mind with thoughts of Johnny seemed to ease the pain.

SCHOOL

The doorbell interrupted my thoughts. It was Casey. She was excited about school so she came early so we could walk together. I was barely dressed and feeling a bit annoyed that I had to spend my days in a stuffy classroom. The education I got in real life was much more meaningful. I wondered if any of the kids at school would see me differently. Could they tell I held a gift that would be the envy of all if they knew of it? Would they recognize my value to society? Suddenly I realized that I really didn't care as much about what other people thought about me. It was a completely new sense of security that I never had before. School was going to be a place I had to go to in between my visits with Jonathan and my dates with Johnny. No longer will it be a place of anxiety and resentment. The Samantha that used to keep her head down in the hallways and act as if I didn't exist was gone, replaced by a shiny new version.

On the half-mile walk to school, I noticed something that I had never noticed before; my school was located next to a cemetery. The cemetery was glowing like a thousand lightning bugs. Even during the day, I could see the glows of wandering spirits. I couldn't take my eyes off it. I could almost feel the spirits energies palpitating from just beyond the entrance. I started counting the lights when Casey interrupted me and asked what I was looking at. I wanted to say, "First class tickets to heaven," but instead I said, "oh nothing, just admiring the scenery." Apparently, that wasn't the right thing to say when looking at headstones. She gave me a look that could kill. I scanned the grounds and instantly knew . . . I had a lot of work to do.

CPSIA information can be obtained
at www.ICGtesting.com
Printed in the USA
FSOW01n0930110615
7836FS